PROJECT BODI

AWAKEN THE POWER OF INSIGHT

D1738995

HOSEIN KOUROS-MEHR

SPECIAL THANKS TO

GORDON LONG

PROLOGUE

I N 2029, ONLY TWO major tech companies were left standing. Google was the biggest company in the world, with a net worth larger than the combined value of 498 other companies in the Fortune 500.

Google fostered an internal culture that produced breakthrough tech products year after year. Its CEO, Shiv Patel, was an oracle of innovation. He unleashed an internal wave of creativity and insight that went deep into the company's fabric. By promoting mindfulness exercises that boosted his employee's insights, Shiv unlocked the mind's inner source of innovation, and he used that power for his company's advantage.

Artificial Intelligence (A.I.) was the theme of the 2020s. Every human task became simplified and more efficient when integrated with A.I. The public demanded to have better and faster A.I., and Google was the primary company to satisfy that demand. Consumers flocked to the latest Google products, whether they were cars, smartphones, smartwatches, or home appliances. With Google Assistant at the center of its platforms, the future was in the hands of machine intelligence.

Shiv Patel was happy with Google's rise to supremacy, but he wanted more. Domination of the tech space was not enough. He wanted to release a game-changing product that would revolutionize society, a product more innovative than the laptop or the smartphone. A breakthrough that would fundamentally alter how human beings interacted with each other and with their environment, the device would augment human reality and enhance the human brain, making it smarter and faster than ever before.

But only if Shiv and the A.I. department could make it work.

PART 1

AWARENESS

1.

D R. SHIV PATEL, GOOGLE'S CEO, sat in the corporate boardroom of the company's global headquarters in Mountain View, California. It was the first Tuesday of September, 2029, which meant another meeting of the Executive Committee, a group of twelve Google senior leaders who met regularly to discuss the company's pipeline and strategic investments.

As the meeting began, Shiv waited patiently to make an unscheduled announcement. There was to be no official record of this presentation. Today he would unveil the company's next major effort, but only after the conclusion of the meeting's scheduled agenda.

On the slate for that month's Executive Committee was "Google Health," the company's latest rollout. Dr. Bethany Andrews, Vice President and head of the company's Artificial Intelligence department, had led the program's development and now she addressed the committee.

"The next Google Health update happens next week," she told them. "The update allows the software to collect data from medical imaging devices like MRIs and CT scanners."

Roger Niles, former CEO of Amazon, cleared his throat. "Dr. Andrews, please remind the committee why we need this software update."

Beth nodded. "Certainly. Google Health determines a patient's condition by analyzing medical information. The more data we collect, the more accurately our A.I algorithms can diagnose. This software update adds medical imaging scanners to our list of Health-compatible devices. Essentially, we are improving Google Health's ability to diagnose."

"And the Quality Control checks have passed?" Roger asked.

"Yes," Beth replied. "I'm happy to report that all QC checks have passed. The update will happen next Friday."

"Impressive," Roger said with a smile. "I'd like to take a minute and recognize Beth's contributions to Google Health. Have the committee members seen this week's issue of *Science*?"

He grabbed his Google Pixel phone and beamed an image onto a wall. It was the cover of *Science* magazine with the headline: "Google Health: Breakthrough of the Year."

The committee erupted in conversation, then applause.

Beth thanked the committee for the acknowledgment. "We've come a long way," she said. "Back in graduate school at MIT, I knew that A.I. would one day change medical practice, and Google Health has made that our new reality. I have to thank the thirty programmers in my department who've worked tirelessly on this advancement."

Shiv Patel laughed. "You're being humble, Beth. This is more than just some advancement. Think about the impact of this product. Google Health can analyze a patient's genome, medical lab results, and now medical imaging data in a matter of seconds. With that information, Google Health can diagnose a patient's disease months before a human physician would recognize any symptoms. Google Health isn't just some advancement; it's a major paradigm shift with profound implications for human health."

Ed Koch, former CEO of Exxon Mobil, waved his finger. "Shiv, be careful with hyperbole. Do you think physicians will be happy to know that we're putting them out of business?"

Shiv rolled his eyes. "Did the stethoscope put physicians out of business? How about the X-ray scan? Ed, I don't think you understand innovation."

"Innovation is a job killer, and this is the worst time in history to be killing jobs."

Shiv made a fist and stared Ed down. Instead of doubling down on his anger, Shiv waited for it to subside.

Compassion is the way to deal with anger.

Shiv unclenched his fists. "Ed, take a look at this survey of physicians who signed up for Health last month. They report overwhelmingly positive outcomes for their practices."

Uncomfortable with the tension, Beth went on to finish her Google Health presentation and then opened the floor to questions. Roger Niles immediately jumped in.

"What is the next big opportunity for Google Health?" Roger asked.

"Good question." Beth thought about it. "I would have to say the next big opportunity is cancer. We have already added a patient's cancer genome into Google Health. We now plan to add the thousands of cancer clinical trials into the platform. Google Health will be able to personalize someone's cancer therapy by referring them to the clinical trial with the maximum benefit."

The room grew silent as they absorbed Beth's comments.

Then Shiv Patel took the floor.

"Thank you, Beth, for the fantastic presentation," Shiv said. "And now I'd like to discuss something off topic."

The team looked at their CEO with intrigue.

Shiv continued. "I want to inform the committee of a new effort within the company. It is a wearable device that will revolutionize our industry."

Eyebrows rose, and the committee members stole glances at one another. This was the first they had heard of a new device.

"The device will be called Google Vision," Shiv said. "It's a pair of smartglasses with more functionality than the smartphone. Google Vision will be so powerful that it will turn the smartphone into obsolete technology."

The room went silent.

"The time is right for a breakthrough that will change the tech landscape. Google Vision will be an elegant device. It will look like a stylish pair of sunglasses, and there won't be an ugly camera or appendage sticking out of the device. The form factor is important. This won't be another Google Glass."

Shiv beamed an image of the Oculus X smartglasses onto a wall.

"Smartglasses have been on the market for a few years now," he continued. "It's a niche market. Today's smartglasses are great for VR, but that's really all they do. Amy, tell the committee about the VR smartglasses on the market."

Amy Fishman, former CEO of Walmart, spoke without hesitation. "Virtual Reality is a consumer favorite. Last holiday season, the Oculus X was a best-selling product, very popular among the young tech-savvy generation. The Oculus is a fun device – a pair of smartglasses that streams videos in VR. This is especially great for live streaming concerts and sporting events; while wearing Oculus you can watch a live concert and feel you're there alongside the concertgoers. It's an immersive experience."

"That's great," Shiv said. "But I don't plan to make just another VR headset. Google Vision will be a new type of smartglasses. It will be the best VR device on the market, but it will do much more than just VR. Google Vision will be the first with Augmented Reality. It will be a VR and AR device in one. Beth, please explain how this will differentiate from our competitors."

Beth's face flushed. She tried to compose herself, waiting patiently for the words to come to her.

"Well," she said, "Augmented Reality refers to technology that superimposes a computer-generated image on your view of the real world, thus providing a composite view. Our goal is to develop Google Vision smartglasses that would allow you to read emails, text messages, and other information directly in your field of view without having to check a smartphone. You could take photos, search on a web browser, or check your calendar through the glasses themselves."

"This will be a revolutionary product," Shiv interrupted. "People will look through the smartglasses and discover the world. They can learn more about anything in their field of view. It will be a fundamentally different experience from the smartphone, which is a utilitarian device. Smartglasses will be a device for discovery. It will take the human mind past its potential and open new avenues. Human memory can be perfected. Human vision and hearing can be augmented. This will truly be a paradigm shift."

Ed Koch shook his head. "Paradigm shifts are dangerous, Shiv. If there's one thing I learned as Exxon Mobil's CEO, it's that new technologies are the death knell for industry leaders. We must be careful, Shiv, especially with Congress hunting down tech companies."

Shiv crossed his arms. "Congress is doing what?"

"You haven't heard? Congress just drafted a new anti-trust bill—Dabney-Page. They want to split Amazon into three companies and restore competition in the retail sector. The public's backlash against Amazon's monopoly is vicious. We may be next on the chopping block, and we should tread carefully."

"Google isn't Amazon," Shiv assured them. "We aren't in the business of global domination. Google's priority is innovation. We are the world's biggest technology company, and we have a social obligation to accelerate technology and push boundaries."

Roger Niles nodded. "I agree. Apple and Microsoft declined because they stopped innovating. We are the world's beacon of progress and we have to carry the torch."

Amy Fishman spoke up. "Roger, that kind of idealistic talk is dangerous. I agree with Ed. We should be careful about the growing populism in the country."

The committee quarreled and split into two camps. For twenty minutes, Shiv and six Executive Committee members advocated for Google Vision, while Ed and his colleagues pushed back against the effort. The shouting gave way to compromise.

Shiv signaled. "Many of you are new to Google, and I understand your hesitation to take risk. As a Googler since 1999, I must remind you that risk-taking is part of Google's DNA. Google Vision is the next leap forward."

Ed shook his head. "Shiv, this isn't the Google of 1999. Times have changed. Innovation just isn't that important for us right now."

"Let's hold a vote," Shiv said defiantly.

Ed grinned. "We will vote only if Google Vision receives the Fast Fail provision."

Shiv looked at Beth and waited for a signal from her, but she remained motionless.

Can she develop Google Vision under Fast Fail pressure?

Shiv pressed forward with the vote, and it was a unanimous decision. He smiled and summarized the final result. "The EC has approved Google Vision with the Fast Fail provision. Do all committee members agree with this outcome?"

Heads nodded, and the room grew silent.

"This project will be given the nickname Bodi," Shiv said. "Project Bodi will be headed by Dr. Andrews."

Beth nodded to acknowledge her CEO's words. "Thanks Shiv. I am deeply honored to be the head of Project Bodi. The A.I. department is ready to take on this new project, which is sure to become a monumental challenge. With Google Health now largely behind us, we can focus all efforts on these new smartglasses."

Shiv opened the floor to questions. The committee members were largely silent, trying to absorb this new information from their CEO. They looked at Beth with respect and envy. The burden of Bodi's development lay on her shoulders.

"I want to remind everyone," Ed said. "Under the Fast Fail provision, we will need to see a working prototype of the Bodi smartglasses in nine weeks from today."

The room grew silent as they fathomed the challenges ahead.

∞ ∞ ∞

On the previous afternoon, Shiv Patel had met with Beth in her office to reveal the details of the new project.

"I appreciate your team's successes on Google Health," he told her. "You're becoming a superstar around here. Is your group ready to take on a new challenge?"

Beth tried to keep the surprise off her face. She knew Shiv thought of her as a rising star in the company, but from his expression, this new project meant a lot to him.

"Of course we are ready for a new effort," Beth replied. "What do you have in mind?"

"It's a device we've built before without much success," Shiv said. "But the time is right for its revival."

Shiv went on to explain his concept for the Google Vision smartglasses and its nickname, Project Bodi.

Beth was intrigued. "Augmented Reality has been a dream of mine. I have no doubt AR smartglasses will be a blockbuster, but do you really think we can solve the challenges for a working device? Augmented Reality has been a pipedream."

Shiv looked Beth in her eyes. "It's time to rise up and innovate. I have confidence in you, Beth. If you harness your team's insights, you will succeed."

"Okay, we will try our best." Beth took in a deep breath. "By the way, what does Project Bodi refer to?"

At Google, products in development often received nicknames to hide their true identity.

Shiv replied, "Bodi is the Sanskrit word for 'awakening.' It's an awareness of the true nature of things. Bodi is the first step needed to awaken the mind's power to innovate."

"Interesting. You're saying there's a way to improve innovation?"

"Yes, exactly," Shiv said. "Every one of us can improve our innovation. It has to do with your subconscious mind. When you tap into your subconscious mind, you will awaken the power of insight and solve any challenge imaginable."

Shiv explained the concepts of awareness and innovation for another fifteen minutes.

"Interesting," Beth said after Shiv's speech. "I'll have to put your ideas to the test, starting with Project Bodi."

Shiv smiled. "I appreciate that. I will unveil the project at tomorrow's Executive Committee meeting. There's a lot riding on this, Beth. You are our superstar, and I'm confident you will make it happen."

Beth left work that day on a cloud of enthusiasm, primed for the committee meeting on Tuesday. She would use Shiv's advice to harness her team's innovation and tackle Project Bodi.

It would be the most difficult undertaking in her young career.

2.

"IT'S A GIANT OCTOPUS!"

Austin Sanders felt the heat from the flaming creature before he actually saw it. He and his friends were walking in the Nevada desert on their way to a concert stage when they felt the intense blast. Turning around, they saw a giant metal octopus with flames shooting out of its tentacles.

"What the hell is that?" Austin said.

"That's El Pulpo!" his friend Cohen said. "I saw that ugly critter at EDC last year."

Austin and his friends Cohen and Matt couldn't stop laughing at the sight of the huge beast. It was a twenty-foot-tall mobile art installation complete with flamethrowers and sound effects. They took out their cellphones and took Snaps, sharing this strange creation with the rest of their social media friends. Their Snaps were liked immediately.

Austin and his friends were at the Burning Man music festival in the middle of the Nevada desert. It was a week-long festival dedicated to art and self-expression, with over 35,000 people in attendance. It was also a hedonistic escapade full of music, drugs, and alcohol. Most attendees

16

were inebriated in some way, and psychedelics were a favorite. It was a psychonaut's paradise. There were multiple music stages playing electronic dance music. There were also art installations, like metal whales emerging from the earth, giant dancing women made of steel, and the flaming octopus.

Austin wanted a group photo in front of the giant octopus, so he reached out to a random passerby.

"Can you take a picture of us?" Austin asked the stranger.

"Yeah, sure," the stranger replied.

Austin handed him the phone and stood with his friends in front of the flaming octopus. It growled and shot a blazing flame out of its tentacles, the perfect moment for a picture. Austin and his friends smiled in the searing heat as the passerby snapped their photo.

"Thanks for the photo!" Austin grabbed his phone from the stranger. It was a surreal snapshot. He quickly uploaded the picture onto Snapchat and Instagram. Austin loved social media and checked his social media platforms every few minutes throughout the day.

The faint sounds of dance music drifted over the desert winds from a stage in the distance. Austin was on his third vodka soda, boosted by an ecstasy pill. He was on another plane of existence. His friends were also tipsy, and it was only 6 PM on the last night of the festival. Tonight would be the celebratory burning of the large wooden man, one of the festival favorites.

"Are you feeling the molly?" Austin asked his friends.

"A little," Matt said. "My jaw's starting to grind."

"Same here."

Cohen pointed. "Hey guys, let's head over to that stage. Looks awesome from here."

As Austin walked, he realized that this was the last night of the festival. Tomorrow he would have to head back to the San Francisco Bay Area and return to the real world.

The thought of returning to work was a buzzkill. He would have to make this night a special one.

"YOLO," Austin told himself. "You only live once."

Austin was a 26-year-old programmer in Google's A.I. Department. Bethany Andrews had hired him straight out of graduate school. He enjoyed his job and had a good relationship with his boss, but lately Austin's focus had turned to music and partying. He lived for music festivals, having attended all the major electronic music events around the world, from the Electronic Daisy Carnival in Las Vegas to the Tomorrowland festival in Belgium.

A few days before Austin set out for the Burning Man festival, Dr. Andrews had met with him to discuss a new effort in the A.I. department.

"Austin, I want you to be involved in Project Bodi," Beth explained to him at his cubicle. "It's our plan to enter the smartglasses space in a big way."

Austin found it difficult to pay attention to his boss. He was busy getting ready for Burning Man.

"I want you to program verbal commands into the Bodi smartglasses," Beth said. "Since your programming background is voice recognition, you're the perfect person for the job."

Austin had earned a master's degree in computer science from the University of Chicago and his thesis was a work of genius – it dealt with the analysis of complex voice recognition.

"Okay, I'll get right on it," Austin replied, before returning to Burning Man preparations.

Austin's assigned task for Project Bodi was a straightforward one, but it came at the wrong time. On the last day at Google before heading off to Nevada, he hastily wrote a software code for voice recognition based on some previous work he had done. He quickly submitted the code to the quality control department for analysis but didn't take the time to check his work before sending it. He was way too excited about Burning Man, and Project Bodi wasn't very high on his list of priorities.

Now on the last night of the Burning Man festival, Austin and his friends were high and drunk. They were walking in the desert on their way to a music stage when they saw something strange in the distance.

Austin squinted against the evening sun and pointed in the distance. "What the hell is that?"

"It looks like two horses," Cohen said.

Austin laughed madly. "You idiot, they have horns on their head. They're freaking unicorns!"

"Well, they're headed in our direction," Matt said.

The three of them stopped walking.

As the unicorns drew closer, it became obvious that they were actually bicycles outfitted to look like unicorns. The wheels and body of the bicycles were covered in white feathers, with giant white horse heads propped up on the handlebars. Each head had a massive unicorn horn projecting out of it. The riders were dressed like Native American shamans. They wore multi-colored feather headdresses with beads, and their faces were painted.

Austin took out his phone and snapped a photo of the unicorn riders. One of the riders spotted the three and started biking towards them.

"Are they coming towards us?" Cohen asked.

Austin was silent. His mind was fuzzy and he was in an altered, dream-like state.

The shamans approached. They stopped their unicorn bicycles just a few feet away. They towered above Austin and his friends, who were now quiet and fearful. Austin put his phone back into his pocket and stared at the shamans.

One of shamans spoke. "Who seeks to be awakened?"

Austin's eyes widened.

Is this real or am I hallucinating?

"You don't seek to be awakened?" the shaman asked. They were about to ride away when Austin spoke up.

"Yes, I'd like to be awakened," Austin said. "But I think I'm awake already."

The shaman came closer to Austin. "If you are already awake," he said, "then you don't need our help."

"But how do I know if I'm awake or not?"

The shaman replied, "If you have to ask yourself that question, then you're probably not awake."

Austin was even more confused, so he decided to give in. "Well, then I wish to be awakened."

One of the shamans got off his bike and walked towards Austin. He looked Austin in the eye and said, "Okay, I can help you."

The shaman reached into his pocket. He blessed Austin with a prayer and placed a small silver bag in his hand.

"Use this to awaken yourself," the shaman said. "And not for any other purpose."

Austin felt a chill down his spine as he accepted the gift. The shaman's words struck deep in his soul. At Burning Man, it was common for people to give gifts to complete strangers. In fact, the atmosphere at the festival was very much one of giving. When a stranger gifted another person, it was also customary to give a thank-you gift in response. Austin reached into his pocket and grabbed his wireless headphones, which he gave to the shaman.

"Thank you," the shaman said to Austin. "Remember, treat this with respect and use it only to awaken yourself." With that, the shamans rode off on their unicorn bicycles.

It was a surreal experience. Austin looked at the small silver bag in his hand. Inside, he found ten strips of paper and a note.

"What did he give you?" Cohen asked.

Austin picked up the note from the silver bag and read it aloud: "Each tab is sacred – only use to awaken yourself."

"Tab?" Cohen asked. "As in LSD tab?"

"Yeah. Ten of them. I've never tried LSD before." He placed them in his pocket and continued walking with his friends to the music stage. The desert winds picked up, blinding them and covering them in sand.

They approached the stage to find thousands of people dancing to electronic music. A giant metal spider looked down on the ravers, the DJ spinning in its mouth. Flames shot from the spider's head. The thumping bass reverberated through the venue and shook Austin to the core. He felt a wave of euphoria come over his body. He closed his eyes and immersed himself in the moment.

Feeling the ecstasy pill wearing off, Austin took the silver bag from his pocket. He took out two tabs and gave them to his friends.

Cohen held the LSD tab. "Are you sure we should do this?"

"YOLO," Austin replied.

"But the shaman said to be careful with it."

Austin rolled his eyes. "Don't be so weak," he said, placing an LSD tab under his tongue.

An hour later, Austin and his friends headed to the Playa for the burning of the wooden man. It was now evening, and a full moon shone. The forty-foot statue stood on a large metal platform, projecting high into the desert sky. It could be seen for miles.

Austin and his friends arrived at the Playa to find a massive crowd of 30,000 people gathered to watch the celebratory burning. Electronic music blasted as people danced in clouds of sand lit with lasers. The voice of a festival organizer came through the speakers, thanking everyone for coming and speaking of the merits of the

Burning Man community. The speaker then counted down the final moments before the fires began.

"You guys feeling the LSD?" Austin asked his friends.

"My stomach's hurting," Cohen said. "What about you?"

Austin shrugged. "I think so. Colors are really popping up and everything's super bright. When I close my eyes, I can see visuals moving around."

"Are you feeling awakened?"

Austin laughed. "I'm already awake. That guy was an idiot." He stumbled around the desert without much awareness of his surroundings. He had mixed alcohol with drugs, which made him hazy and incoherent.

Suddenly there was an explosion, and the huge wooden man went up in flames. Austin and his friends watched in awe as the flames shot into the sky. They took out their smartphones and snapped photos of the scene, which they shared on multiple social medial platforms. There was a silence as the flames overtook the burning man. People realized that the festival would be over soon.

Austin sighed. "Can't believe I have to be back to work. That and the come-down. So depressing."

"Let's keep the party going!" Matt said. "Don't be a downer, Austin. YOLO!"

Soon after the burning man's flames died down, Austin and his friends headed back to their RV on the festival campgrounds. They stayed up until 3 AM, trying to avoid the inevitable conclusion of the festival.

The next morning, they drove back to the San Francisco Bay Area.

3.

"**G**OOD MORNING, BETH. It's going to be a cool day with a high of 62 degrees."

Beth smiled as she got into her Google SUV on a cool September morning. Her car's A.I. greeted her every morning and gave her the weather forecast for the day. She had recently changed her car A.I.'s name to "Cooper," having grown tired of "Linda." Her A.I., now with a new male name, still spoke to her in a female voice.

"Hey, Cooper," Beth said to her car. "Can you speak to me in a male British accent?"

"Why, of course," her car replied with a male British accent.

"Can you make me a British breakfast?" Beth asked with a laugh.

"Don't be silly," Cooper responded.

Beth looked into her rear-view mirror and saw dark bags under her eyes. She had not slept well that night.

"Cooper, please drive me to work."

"Certainly."

As Beth's Google SUV drove itself to work that morning, she grabbed makeup from her purse and concealed the bags under her eyes. She had slept for only two hours that night. Her three-year-old daughter Gabriella had complained of an earache and couldn't sleep.

"Cooper, what's the cause of ear ache in a three-year old child?"

"The most common cause of ear ache in a three-year-old child is bacterial infection. It should be treated by oral antibiotics prescribed by a physician."

Beth had suspected an infection. Her daughter felt warm and was fussy all night. Beth's husband Reza had taken Gabriella to the pediatric urgent care clinic early that morning. Beth felt fortunate that Reza took control of the matter. Reza was a self-employed tech entrepreneur who worked from home, which gave Beth the flexibility she needed to run Google's most important department.

Cooper soon drove the car to Mountain View and pulled up to Google's main entrance. Beth waved and smiled to Lou, the parking attendant, as her car drove itself into Parking Lot A for another day of work.

"Good morning, Dr. Beth," Lou said with a smile.

Beth waved back. "Good morning, Lou."

Beth didn't like to be called "Dr. Beth" or "Dr. Andrews" because she felt that it glorified her ego, preferring just "Beth." Cooper drove the car into the empty parking lot, arriving at a reserved parking spot: "Vice President, Dr. Andrews." Here was another reminder of her title. Beth tried to be a humble person at all times; she felt that over-confidence or entitlement were negative qualities that stifled innovation. To be fair, her title was something not easily overlooked at a major corporation like Google. She was, after all, a superstar in a company of stars.

Bethany was head of Google's A.I. department, and she was the company's youngest Vice President. She had earned a Ph.D. in Artificial Intelligence from MIT before joining Google as a lead programmer. In just six years at Google, she had climbed the ranks from lead programmer to Manager, Senior Manager, and finally to Vice President. Only a select few had accomplished such a feat.

As Beth removed her belongings from her car and headed to work, she noticed that the cherry trees along the walkway had blossomed. All along the walkway, there were pink and white blooms contrasting vibrantly with the blue sky. Beth stopped for a second to take in the view.

Be here now.

Her philosophy was to be aware of the present moment, not to be distracted by memories of the past or thoughts of the future. She closed her eyes and focused her attention on the smell of the cherry trees, giving her a few moments of relaxation. She then continued to her office.

Beth was a morning person and preferred to arrive at work before most employees had awoken. She preferred to work when her mind was clear, which was usually early in the morning. She grabbed a coffee and entered her office, then turned on her computer. In just a few seconds, the barrage of information appeared on her computer screen – 104 emails, 5 instant messages, 3 voicemails, and countless tweets, posts, friend requests, and direct messages on multiple social media platforms. Deciding not to waste her time on anything trivial, she scanned her email for anything of importance.

She spotted an email with the subject: "Project Bodi: Quality check fail (!)" Beth read the email and her mood turned somber.

"Project Bodi – Update V1.2 – Voice Command Integration. Twelve fatal errors in code, including syntactic errors, missing command errors, functionality errors, and control flow errors. Major revision required."

Beth cringed. Her team's latest programming efforts were a failure. Project Bodi was now the lead project in her A.I. department, and the V1.2 software update attempted to integrate voice commands into the operating system so that you could control the smartglasses with your own voice.

The errors in the code were all in Bodi's voice commands, and there was one programmer in charge of writing that code – Austin Sanders. The flaws in the code prevented it from integrating with Bodi's other functionalities, causing the software to crash.

Beth had asked Austin to check his code for errors, but clearly Austin had not paid attention to his boss's request.

With clenched fists, Beth got up and dashed to Austin's cubicle. She found him listening to music on his headphones. He had just returned from a four-day vacation. Beth tapped him on the shoulder, startling him.

Austin turned around and winced at the sight of his boss. He looked tired and his eyes were red, as if he hadn't slept for days. "Good morning, Dr. Andrews."

"Hi Austin. Have you seen the QC email on Bodi?"

Austin's face flushed. He had not yet checked his work email, having spent the morning digging through social media posts about Burning Man.

"We're in trouble," Beth said. "The voice recognition code has a number of fatal flaws. Did you check your code before submitting it to QC?"

"I didn't realize that." He turned around and quickly closed his social media feed. "I'll have a new version before our team meeting on Wednesday."

Beth sighed. There was no time to yell at him for his mistakes. "Austin, I'm losing confidence in you. You said you needed two days off last week to clear your mind. I hope it worked. You'll have to start over from scratch."

Beth could not stand to look at Austin any longer. She spun around and headed back to her office, slamming the door behind her. She paced back and forth, anxiously plotting her next move.

There was a knock on the door, and her administrative assistant, Sara, walked in.

"Everything okay?" Sara asked.

"We're in trouble," Beth replied. "Project Bodi is failing."

"Failing? I thought the department was making solid progress."

Beth sat and grabbed her coffee. "Well, it's been three weeks since Shiv gave us this project. We've managed to create an early prototype with VR functionality, which is great, but it's just not enough."

Sara shrugged. "Seems like a lot of progress to me! You've developed VR smartglasses in only three weeks."

Beth sighed. "Yeah, the VR is great, but that's not the issue."

Beth unlocked a drawer and took out a prototype of the Bodi smartglasses from the desk. It was a sleek pair of sunglasses with small speakers on the earpieces.

Sara's jaw dropped when she handled the smartglasses. "They're so light!"

"Try them on. For now, you can switch between Off Mode and VR Mode by tapping on the side of the glasses. In one instant, you're looking around at your natural surroundings, and then when you tap the glasses you'll switch to VR Mode and watch videos in high-definition virtual reality. You can watch the Super Bowl and feel you're there in person. You can look anywhere on the field, check the scoreboard, or look at the fans around you and feel their experience."

Beth showed Sara how to operate the device. "In VR mode, you can also watch movies, TV shows, and music videos in Virtual Reality. It's the closest thing to being a part of a film or TV show."

Sara's eyes lit up. "I can't wait to buy one of these! I'm so proud of you, Beth."

Beth shook her head. "Thanks Sara, but the VR features aren't enough. Just as Shiv told us, there's already significant competition in the VR space, and our competitors will launch similar products soon. We need to give Bodi an edge. I'm trying to program Augmented Reality into Bodi's operating system, and that's where we're failing."

Sara hesitated. "...And... Augmented Reality will do what, again?"

Beth laughed. "There are no dumb questions, Sara. With Augmented Reality, you will see your natural environment as you would through a pair of sunglasses but with data entering your field of view in real time. We want to program thousands of capabilities into Bodi – messaging, music streaming, shopping, and much more. We want to program AR as the third mode in the device. But so far, the AR functionality is just a fantasy."

"Why is Augmented Reality so difficult to program, Beth?" Sara asked.

"It's a command issue. Let's say you're wearing the smartglasses and you want to send a text message. What's the best command to do that?"

Sara shrugged her shoulders.

"One way is through verbal commands," Beth said. "You can talk to Google Assistant and she will complete the task for you. I asked Austin to program verbal commands for Bodi, but his coding was a colossal failure and it crashed our latest software update."

"So it's Austin's fault?"

"Yes, exactly. I've been frustrated by Austin recently. He was my first hire, and he was an enthusiastic employee at the start. But a few months in, he became really distracted. Anytime I walk over to his cubicle, I find him on Snapchat or Wired. He never seems to be doing any work."

Sara hesitated. "...I've...noticed he's been coming to work late and leaving early."

Beth grew upset. "That's good to know, Sara. Can you please contact Karen Park in HR? I'd like to talk to her about Austin."

"Will do."

"And Sara?"

The Assistant turned in the doorway.

"Thank you. It really helps when I vent to you."

Sara nodded and went about her business.

∞ ∞ ∞

After several morning meetings, Beth's level of stress continued to increase. In the three weeks since the Executive Committee meeting, her team had made very little progress on Augmented Reality. In order to meet the nine-week deadline, she would have to start innovating immediately. But so far, there was no innovation from the team.

Beth panicked.

What if we can't deliver a working prototype?

Fear and anxiety flooded Beth's mind. She knew she had to calm herself down.

Be here now.

She wanted to clear her mind and start the day over. Somehow, she would have to find a solution for Bodi that did not involve Austin Sanders.

I could write the code myself...no, that would take too long. I need a faster way.

Beth wanted to calm her mind as soon as possible. She found a break room and locked the door behind her. Sitting in a leather chair, she began a ten-minute breathing exercise. She slowly inhaled for a few seconds, paused, and then exhaled for a few seconds. She tried to focus on her breathing, but thoughts of panic and frustration entered her mind. She worried about Project Bodi. She felt the disappointment from not meeting the project deadline.

Instead of reacting to the feelings of panic and anxiety, Beth observed the feelings, watching them from a distance, almost like watching the cherry blossom trees earlier in the day. As soon as she observed one anxious thought, another one entered her mind. She then observed this new thought, watching it from a distance. By developing awareness of the thoughts, Beth simply watched as the thoughts entered and exited her mind. The thoughts of panic and frustration subsided, and she entered the present state.

Quiet the mind, and the soul will speak.

Beth then remembered Shiv's advice about harnessing innovation. She practiced a mindfulness exercise to awaken her mind's intuition. As Shiv had explained, if she tapped into her subconscious mind, the path forward would become obvious.

Beth's heart began to beat normally and time returned to its normal pace. Although she was not any closer to solving Bodi's problems, she was now calm and at ease. Shiv had said that the subconscious mind delivered deep insights when the mind was at peace.

The solutions to Bodi's challenges remained elusive, but Beth was confident she could salvage the project. She took an extended break and went for an afternoon walk around the campus to clear her mind.

Several hours later, Beth left the office for the day and marveled at the cherry blossoms on her walk back to the parking lot. She entered her car.

"Good afternoon, Beth."

"Hi, Cooper. Please take me home."

The Google car drove itself to the parking exit, where Beth said goodbye to Lou and then headed back home to Menlo Park. Her car merged onto the 101 Freeway and hit severe traffic. Her navigation notified her of an accident three miles ahead. Stuck on the freeway with nowhere to go, Beth turned on her radio and reflected on her day.

She flipped through several stations and on came Thievery Corporation, one of her favorite bands. It was actually one of her favorite songs that played – "Lebanese Blonde." It reminded her of a concert she attended with her high school boyfriend. She grew nostalgic, remembering the freedom of youth. She missed being carefree and having the time and energy to discover the world. She had such wonderful memories of her childhood.

Then, out of nowhere, Beth had a deep insight.

She knew how to solve Bodi. It was as if the idea had fallen from the sky. The simplicity of the solution was stunning.

Beth had tasked Austin Sanders to program Bodi's Augmented Reality because of his background in voice recognition. After all, Bodi's functions would be guided by your voice commands.

Instead of voice, what if your eyes guided Bodi's commands?

Beth knew that the eyes could run Bodi's programs much faster and more efficiently than voice. While wearing Bodi, if you wanted to learn about a nearby restaurant, you would look directly at the restaurant and open a tab with more information. You would read reviews of the restaurant, check the menu, and make a dinner reservation through the smartglasses.

With eye-tracking and artificial intelligence, the eyes can be trained to run Bodi's software.

Beth smiled as she pulled up to her home in Menlo Park. She parked the car and grabbed her belongings, rushing to see her family.

"Look Gabriella, Mommy's home!" Reza said as the door opened.

"Hi sweetie pie," Beth said, hugging her daughter tightly. "How's her ear pain?"

"She's much better now," Reza replied. "How was your day?"

"It was good. I just had a brilliant idea for our lead project. I can't wait to get back to my team and tell them about it."

Reza hugged his wife. "I'm proud of you. Sounds like you had a great day."

"Not exactly," Beth said. "There's someone on my team who nearly ruined it. He's very distracted and can't be trusted with serious responsibility. I'll have to demote him and replace him with someone from our visual recognition team."

4.

SHIV PATEL LOOKED AT THE TIME and realized he was running late for work. He had made breakfast for his daughters, but they were nowhere to be found.

"Tara and Malia!" he yelled. "Hurry down for breakfast!"

Shiv Patel loved to make breakfast for his daughters. He had a butler and several caregivers who took care of his daughters at their sprawling home in the San Francisco Marina district, but he preferred to cook breakfast himself. It was something he did daily ever since his wife had passed away from pancreatic cancer a few years ago. Cooking breakfast was a chance to interact with his daughters before they went off to school.

"Coming!" he heard a shout from upstairs. It was Malia. A few minutes later, Shiv's daughters came running downstairs, bickering with each other.

"Tara took my brush!" Malia yelled.

"Girls, calm down and sit at the table."

"But I'm in a hurry, Dad."

Shiv took a deep breath. "Malia, you know you shouldn't eat when you're in a rush. Please sit and let's have a pleasant breakfast together."

Shiv spent a few minutes having breakfast with his daughters, then remembered he had a meeting with Google's board of directors in 30 minutes. He asked his caregiver, Maria, to take over. Shiv kissed the girls goodbye for the day and headed to his elevator. A few seconds later, he was on the roof deck of his home.

Shiv headed to his Google Drone parked on the rooftop helipad. The Google Drone self-driving helicopter had become a favorite among the tech elite, but only a handful of executives were able to purchase one. San Francisco had recently enacted a law requiring self-driving helicopters to be parked on large rooftop helipads and monitored with public air-traffic equipment. The costs were prohibitive, and most executives didn't have any space to build a helipad.

"Good morning, Shiv," his helicopter's A.I. said to him.

"Hi Anaya," Shiv responded. "Please get me to work as soon as possible. I have a board meeting in thirty minutes."

"You will make it on time," Anaya said.

The engines turned on and the massive blades spun. The helicopter lifted off the ground and headed south towards Mountain View. Shiv looked at the beautiful city of San Francisco below him. The Bay Bridge was jammed with traffic at that hour. Soon the entire San Francisco Bay was visible.

Shiv used his morning commute as a time to practice mindfulness meditation. He closed his eyes and took several deep breaths, calming his mind. He brought his attention to the present moment, focusing on any sounds or sensations. Soon he entered a state of full awareness.

After a few minutes, he opened his eyes and felt a deep sense of calm. His mind was at ease.

Then he remembered something. "Anaya, I'd like to dictate a document."

"Okay. Is this a new or existing document?"

"New."

"What is the title of the document?"

Shiv thought about it for a few seconds. "Awaken the Power of Insight."

A blank screen appeared on the Drone's tablet computer, the document's title at the top.

Shiv was in the process of writing an operating manual for new Google employees. His Human Resources staff had already drafted most of the manual, discussing matters related to corporate culture, housing, goals, etc. Shiv wanted to include a personal letter helping his new employees foster their innovation and unleash their mind's full potential.

He had an insight as to what the document should look like.

"Dear Google employee," Shiv said. The text appeared on the tablet as he spoke. "Welcome to Google. I hope that your employment here is rewarding and exhilarating. We have high expectations for your success."

Shiv looked at his dictation and then stared at the horizon. He imagined the challenges and stresses of the new Google employee, whose average age was twenty-four.

Shiv collected his thoughts. "In this document, I will describe a process for enhancing your creativity and innovation. It is a method I have used in my own life with great results, one that I have encouraged others at Google to use."

Shiv paused and stretched his arms and legs. He took a deep breath and gazed at the Golden Gate Bridge, glistening in the morning sun. Suddenly he felt a wave of energy come over him.

"At Google, you will confront challenges on a daily basis. Often when you face a difficult problem that you cannot solve, the solution may appear to you later in the day when you are relaxed and your mind is calm. You may be exercising when you recall your problem, and the solution becomes obvious. It feels magical, as if a higher power has delivered a gift of insight. How did this happen? Was it by chance that the solution presented itself? Why do the solutions to our most difficult problems appear to us later when our minds are relaxed? And how can we receive more of these insights throughout the day?"

Shiv stared at his document. "Anaya, please analyze the style of what I've written so far."

After a brief lag, the AI put up a graph on the screen. "Document correlates 73 percent with the genre *Self-Help Books*."

Shiv threw his hands in the air. He laughed at the thought of a new Google employee reading a self-help document written by his company's CEO.

Shiv thought back on his first day at Google. He was a twenty-five-year-old programmer with a Caltech Ph.D. when he started working there as a lead programmer. His first manager at Google had taken a hands-off approach, giving Shiv freedom to pursue anything. This seemed great at first, but the lack of direction eventually led to boredom and frustration. Shiv drifted aimlessly during his first few years on the job. He was unproductive and soon became depressed.

I wish I had been given more direction as a new hire. I know many new Google employees suffer the same issues I once faced.

"Anaya, continue document."

"Please go ahead."

"When you come across a challenge, your conscious mind will try to solve the problem in several different ways. It may access memories of similar situations you faced in the past, looking for solutions you found previously. It may try to deconstruct the problem or approach it from different viewpoints. However, if the problem you face is particularly difficult, the conscious mind may not be able to find a solution.

"When the conscious mind tries to solve a difficult problem and cannot find a solution, it sends that problem to the subconscious mind, which continues to search for a solution even though you are not aware. The subconscious mind is the true powerhouse of your brain, able to solve complex challenges with its unlimited set of resources. It contains all of your memories and all of the knowledge you have learned since you were a toddler. It uses this vast repository of knowledge to solve your daily problems without any awareness on your part."

A beep from the console told Shiv he was a few minutes away from Mountain View. He looked at the document and glanced at the title: "Awaken the Power of Insight."

"When the subconscious mind solves one of your challenging problems, it delivers the solution to you in the form of an insight. These insights are gifts for solving your problems and improving your life. Insights can make you profoundly successful and productive. You can become innovative, wealthy, and powerful if you can learn to harness the insights from your subconscious mind. When you realize the power of your subconscious mind, you can be at ease knowing there is a superior force guiding you through your life."

Shiv finished his dictation just as his helicopter descended into Google Headquarters in Mountain View. The campus was sprawling. Below him was a helipad with five other Google Drones. As his helicopter descended, he looked up and saw the moon in the daytime sky. As he was thinking about the conscious and subconscious minds, an idea came to him, inspired by the sight of moon lying in the vastness of the blue sky.

As Shiv's Drone landed, he grabbed his belongings and hurried to a corporate building where his meeting was underway.

∞ ∞ ∞

Three hours later, Shiv left the meeting and headed to his office on the top floor of Google's tallest building.

Dora, his secretary, greeted him. "Dr. Patel, your 11:00 AM meeting was just cancelled."

"Finally, an hour to relax!"

He walked into his office, which looked like a massive Lake Tahoe cabin with high ceilings and oak walls. There was a sweeping view of Silicon Valley from the tall windows. Shiv walked to his desk and grabbed a tablet computer.

"Anaya," Shiv said. The A.I. was integrated into all of Shiv's devices, including his smartphone, smartwatch, tablets, cars, and helicopter. He could seamlessly transition between devices. It was an ecosystem operated by artificial intelligence.

"Yes, Shiv," Anaya replied from the tablet.

"I'd like to continue editing my last document."

"The document 'Awaken the Power of Insight'?"

"Yes."

Shiv remembered the moon in the sky. It was a perfect analogy for the conscious and subconscious minds. The moon lay in the vast blue sky just as the conscious mind was embedded in the infinite subconscious mind.

Shiv grabbed a stylus pen and drew a circle on his tablet. "Anaya, please add this figure to my document."

"What is the name of the figure?"

Shiv contemplated. "A Model of the Mind."

38

Subconscious Mind

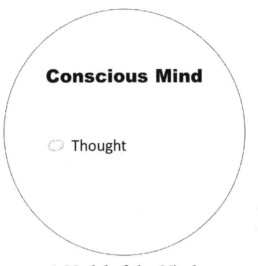

A Model of the Mind

"Insights from our subconscious mind are valuable tools in our lives. To understand how insights occur, let's imagine that our conscious mind is a circle. Within this circle are the thoughts, memories, and emotions in our current awareness. For instance, a thought that enters our conscious mind is a point in the circle. Throughout the day, many hundreds of these points appear in our circle of consciousness.

"If the area within the circle is the conscious mind, then the area outside of the circle represents the subconscious mind. These two parts of the mind communicate all the time. The subconscious is where difficult problems are solved. All of our knowledge, thought, and experience are stored in the vastness of the subconscious. If we harness the infinite power of the subconscious mind, we are capable of extraordinary achievements."

Shiv looked at his "Model of the Mind" and had an idea. "Anaya, I'd like to add a new section to this document."

"What is the title of the new section?"

"How Insights Develop."

A new sub-heading appeared on the screen. "Anaya, can you copy the last figure and place it in this section?"

The "Model of the Mind" appeared. Shiv added two points and two lines and then replaced the figure's title with a new one, calling it "The Development of Insight."

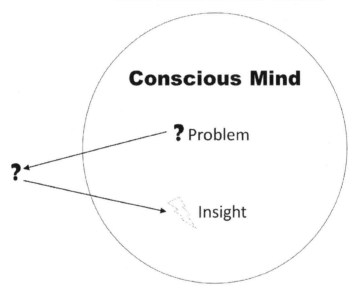

The Development of Insight

"Let's take the example of a difficult problem that we face in our day at Google. When we become aware of this problem, it appears as a point within our circle. Our conscious mind tries to solve the problem without success, so it sends the problem over to our subconscious mind. This is a line going from inside the circle to the outer area. When the subconscious mind solves the problem, it sends the solution back into the conscious mind in the form of an insight."

Shiv looked at his tablet. He had a working model for the conscious and subconscious minds, and now he had a model for insight and innovation.

"Insights delivered from the subconscious mind happen spontaneously, but the environment of the mind will influence the communication of these insights. In general, a mind that is aware and mindful will receive more insights from the subconscious mind. There are mental exercises you can practice to improve your awareness and mindfulness. These exercises will help you tap into your subconscious mind, and you will become more innovative. In this way, you can awaken the power of insight."

Shiv reviewed his document. "Anaya, please send this document to Harry in HR."

"Would you like to include a message to Harry?"

Shiv thought about it. "Hi Harry, please include this document in our new Google employee welcome packet. It's a work in progress, so please edit and make a more palatable version for our young audience."

"Ready to send the email?" Anaya asked.

Shiv looked at the document one last time. "No. Don't send it yet. I'd like to add something."

"Please proceed with addition."

"In contrast to the focused mind, the distracted mind has a difficult time receiving insights from the subconscious mind. This is because the distracted mind has poor communication between the conscious and subconscious minds. The answers to difficult problems are discovered by the subconscious mind, but in a distracted mind these answers aren't delivered to the conscious mind. So the distracted mind finds itself unable to solve the problems it faces."

With that, Shiv emailed the document to the Human Resources department for their review.

5.

"MOLLY, CAN YOU GET ME some molly?"
"I'm afraid I can't do that, Austin."

Austin Sanders sat at his cubicle at Google Headquarters in Mountain View. He was still recovering from the Burning Man Festival. Depressed and moody, he suffered from a post-ecstasy crash.

"Molly, how long have I been sitting here?" he asked his A.I.

"Almost an hour."

Austin rolled his eyes. "Molly, open my Wired app."

That morning Austin was trying to re-program voice recognition features for Project Bodi. It should have been a straightforward coding process, but Austin was not very focused.

Instead of working, Austin flipped through Wired, a new social media app that combined photos and videos from Snapchat, Instagram, and other apps. It was a new kind of social media experience, very popular among teenagers.

"Molly, open Wired photos from Burning Man."

Austin smiled as he reflected on his Burning Man trip. His ears were still ringing and his body was tired, but he still basked in the afterglow of the festival.

What an amazing experience!

Sitting in his cubicle, Austin barely remembered taking some of the photos he was seeing on Wired: shots of a giant metal octopus with flames shooting out of its arms, flamethrowers in a Moroccan villa complete with camels and belly dancers, and extraterrestrial bicycle riders dressed in alien costumes. There were hundreds of psychedelic artworks and sculptures. Burning Man had been an epic event.

"Molly, what is the next EDM event around here?" Austin asked.

"There's an event at the Shoreline Amphitheatre tomorrow night."

"Who's headlining?"

"DJ 3LAU."

His eyes lit up.

My favorite DJ!

Austin was not the stereotypical introspective programmer who lacked a social life. In fact, he was a raging extrovert. He loved electronic dance music, and he had a large group of friends that traveled with him to all the major electronic music festivals throughout the world. Last year, he used his company bonus to book a trip to the Tomorrowland festival in Belgium. It was a three-night hedonistic escapade full of drugs and partying. The festival was like Disneyland but with drugs – there were amusement rides, fairytale themed stages, and psychedelic neon gardens.

"Hey, Austin," said a voice, interrupting his thoughts. It was Beth.

Austin quickly closed his Wired feed and turned around to look at his boss, overcome by fear. "Good morning, Dr. Andrews."

"Austin, I've been upset by your recent production. I've asked Karen Park in HR to have a discussion with you about your work here at Google."

Austin's heart raced. He couldn't believe what he was hearing. He was silent and avoided eye contact.

"I've decided to reorganize the Bodi team," Beth said to him. "Some folks from the visuals group will be joining us. You will stay on but in a different capacity. I'll explain later."

With that, Beth walked away, leaving Austin confused. "Reorganize" was never a good word at a company like Google.

Am I in trouble?

He quickly logged on to his work email to look for any clues about Bodi. Before he got very far, he came across an email about a happy hour event later that day. The theme of the happy hour was "Spring Break," and the attire was casual.

Am I wearing the right clothes for happy hour?

Google was famous for its happy hours. They were terrific networking opportunities and for Austin a great way to meet girls.

Just then, Austin received a notification about one of the stocks in his portfolio, MNK pharmaceuticals. They had just received breakthrough designation for their prostate cancer drug. The stock was up 6% in the last hour.

"Molly, open my stock trading account," he said, before logging on to his online brokerage account to buy some more stock.

As he was completing the stock purchase, he received a text from Cohen, his Burning Man compatriot. "How you feelin' bro?"

Austin smiled. "Still rollin' lol," he texted back.

"Remember this beast?" Cohen texted the picture of the three of them standing in front of the flaming octopus.

"That thing was hot and ugly!"

Austin thought back to Burning Man and smiled even more. He logged onto Wired to see more photos from Burning Man. He treasured the memories from the desert. The artwork at Burning Man was unlike anything he'd seen before: a 20-foot-tall metal sculpture of a dancing woman, a tractor-trailer suspended in mid-air attached to another tractor-trailer on the ground, a large metal blue whale emerging from the earth. Burning Man had been a once-in-a lifetime event.

Partying at Burning Man had been one of Austin's lifelong dreams, but so was working for Google. "Work hard, play hard" was his motto. He didn't believe he actually had to work hard, because he was gifted with genius. He had been among the top of his high school graduating class in Connecticut and attended Brown University on a scholarship. After college, he went to the University of Chicago for a master's degree in voice recognition analysis, graduating with honors. He didn't have to study hard during college or graduate school, spending most of this time playing video games or chatting on social media. Things just came easily for him.

After completing his master's program, Austin was recruited by Google and hired as a lead programmer. It was a dream to work at Google, the world's most valued tech company. He worked on Google Health's voice recognition functionality and made a few contributions to the platform. Austin had all the qualifications to be a successful Googler.

However, Austin was never promoted at Google, and he never received any awards. He could not figure out why.

It's probably politics, or maybe my appearance that's holding me back.

Deep down Austin really wanted to be a successful programmer, and he very much wanted a job promotion. Somehow, it proved elusive.

∞ ∞ ∞

Later that day, the A.I. Department met to discuss updates on Project Bodi. Beth had scheduled an urgent meeting, and all thirty employees in her department showed up, including Austin.

Beth started the meeting without hesitation. She stood up and addressed her team. "I've decided to fundamentally change Bodi's operating system. We will no longer use voice commands in Bodi's primary interface."

Most team members sat upright with keen interest.

"Bodi's primary interface will now be guided by eye tracking," she said. "The smartglasses will track your eyes to guide its decision making."

Paul Sawyers, a lead programmer in the department, raised his hand. "That's going to be really difficult to program."

"Yes, Paul, I know that. We will need to develop software that for the first time in history will operate through visual commands. It will be a challenge. There are gaps in our programming knowledge standing in the way. I need all of you to think differently and innovate. We have only one shot at this."

The room grew silent.

"There will also be some changes to the team," Beth continued. "I've asked some folks from the visual recognition team to join our group."

Beth pointed to three programmers and asked them to introduce themselves. Each programmer stood up and briefly discussed his background with the rest of the team.

"I became a Googler after the Microsoft merger last year. I've mostly worked on VR gaming."

"My background is hardware, working on VR for the Pixel headset."

"I'm Jose but you can call me Mr. Jose." The room erupted in laughter. "I developed VR holograms at Google X, and so I can't really say much more about it."

Beth stood. "Thank you for the introductions. We will also have a fourth new team member with a background in voice recognition joining us next week. Austin Sanders will now be a backup programmer and have less capacity on the team."

Austin tensed. He could not believe what he was hearing.

Beth's demoting me to backup programmer?

Everyone turned to Austin. He nodded awkwardly and looked away.

This must be reverse sexism. Or maybe it's politics.

Austin grew angry. Beth continued the meeting, but he could no longer pay attention to her.

I can't stand this anymore. I need to switch departments, or maybe I should just leave this company!

Austin grabbed his phone and sent an instant message to Cohen. "Are you free tomorrow night?"

"Yeah, what's up?"

"3LAU at Shoreline!"

":)"

"VIP Tickets? I'll buy one for you."

"I'm in!"

Austin smiled, forgetting about Project Bodi and Beth.

∞ ∞ ∞

The following night, Austin and his friends headed to Shoreline Amphitheatre for the music festival headlined by DJ 3LAU.

"This is epic," Austin said as they entered the Amphitheatre. Beyond a concession stand, a massive outdoor concert stage blasted electronic dance music.

"Thanks for inviting us," Cohen said. Like his friends, he wore fluorescent shorts, sneakers, and a wig. Their costume theme was "80s big hair."

Austin looked around the venue. He spotted a grassy field in the back where youngsters were free to dance and take their drugs. Most of the concertgoers wore costumes and backpacks that were perfect for smuggling contraband.

Drugs had become an integral part of the electronic dance music scene. The chemicals were getting more and more potent, and now toxic contaminants were appearing in them. Most of the drug users had no idea what they were ingesting. A few months earlier at a music festival in Belgium, several young ravers had died after ingesting ecstasy pills laced with PMA, a neurotoxic compound. Afraid of the backlash, festival promoters enforced a zero tolerance policy for drug possession. But this had no effect on drug use at the festivals. Promoters then allowed drug testing on festival grounds, so that ravers could be certain their drugs weren't tainted by toxic contaminants.

Austin and his friends always tested their drugs with kits they purchased online. Tonight they were taking molly, also known as ecstasy, a popular street drug at electronic music festivals. Austin's pills contained 100% pure MDMA, an amphetamine and the active compound in molly.

Austin and his friends headed to the back of the amphitheater.

"When is 3LAU coming on?" Austin asked.

"About an hour," Matt said.

"Perfect. I'm gonna take some molly. You guys want some?"

Cohen hesitated. "No, I'm good. I'm still recovering from Burning Man."

Austin turned to Matt. "Buddy? This is the perfect time. We'll be peaking right when 3LAU comes on."

Matt nodded and took a pill from Austin. They swallowed the pills and chased them with vodka.

"I really needed this," Austin said to his friends. "I had a really bad week at work. My boss is a bitch."

Austin stared at the main stage and grinned. There was a giant screen playing psychedelic videos, along with dancers, lasers, and smoke that heightened the electronic music. It was a sensory climax.

An hour later, Austin and his friends made their way to the front of the concert stage. He felt a wave of nausea, his head throbbing.

He nudged Cohen. "The molly is kicking in. My jaw feels heavy." He began to grind his teeth.

As 3LAU came on stage and played his set, Austin felt a strong wave of euphoria reverberate through his mind and body.

Standing in a sea of ravers, Austin's jaw dropped as the headliner played his first song. The music sounded incredibly amazing, and the bass shook the entire venue. Every bone in Austin's body vibrated in harmony with the music. The flashing lights from the mainstage hypnotized him. It felt better than sex.

Austin hugged his friends. "Thank you guys for being in my life."

"We should always stay friends," Matt told him.

"You guys will be my groomsmen," Austin slurred.

Cohen laughed. "You don't even have a girlfriend!"

Austin felt a deep appreciation for his friends, and he felt lucky to be alive. The future seemed limitless at that moment.

∞ ∞ ∞

The next morning, Austin awoke with a throbbing headache; his jaw was sore and his eyes were full of sand.

He looked at his alarm clock. "Two hours sleep. Gaahh!" He reached for the Advil.

"Should've drunk more water," he told himself. "Molly, remind me to drink more water before bed."

"Noted," his A.I. replied.

49

Austin considered calling in sick that day, but then he remembered his demotion on Project Bodi. He knew he couldn't afford to miss another day of work. Slowly he climbed out of bed and made his way to the restroom, then rushed into the bathroom to vomit. He puked everything he had eaten the night before.

Somehow, Austin managed to put on his clothing and drive to work, arriving at 10 AM. His cubicle was disorganized and full of clutter, just like his state of mind. He drank a double espresso and checked his work emails. Then an instant message popped up on his computer screen.

The message was from Karen Park, a staff member in the human resources department. In charge of layoffs and department reorganizations, Karen was notoriously called "The HR Gunner."

"Mr. Sanders," the note said. "Please join Beth and me in meeting room B1-12 at 10:30 AM."

Austin's heart sank. He tensed up and put his head in his hands.

I can't believe this is happening.

Several minutes later, he slowly made his way to B1-12, trembling in fear. He peeked into the meeting room. Karen and Beth sat there, stern and quiet. Austin's heart pounded in his chest. He waited outside for a few minutes to gather himself. Then he entered the meeting room.

"Good morning, Mr. Sanders," Karen Park said. "Please have a seat."

Austin sat at the table and said nothing.

"We want to discuss your work here at Google," Karen continued. "How would you rate your overall work performance?"

Austin hesitated, his heart still pounding. "...Things are going well."

Karen interrupted. "We have documented a number of mistakes in your work, and lately you have been missing meetings. We've decided to put you on a probation period. For the next three months, we will closely monitor your work. If this poor performance continues, we will have no choice but to terminate your employment at the end of the probation."

Karen handed Austin several handouts, including an "Employment Contract" and a "Probationary Review" form.

Austin grew pale, panicking. The nausea worsened and he feared not being able to stand after the meeting. Karen spoke for another ten minutes and he tried hard to focus, but his mind was foggy from the drugs. For the first time, he came face to face with failure. Hopelessness set in.

"Any questions, Mr. Sanders?" Karen asked.

Austin shook his head. After a silent period, Karen grabbed her belongings and left the room. He and Beth were now alone.

"Austin, I don't know what's going on with you," Beth said. "I know you are a smart guy; I'm the one who hired you. But lately your performance has stalled."

Austin still did not look into Beth's eyes.

"When you first joined Google, I thought we had a wonderful work relationship. You were productive and you even made some contributions to Google Health. It was a great experience for someone fresh out of graduate school. Somehow along the way, you lost your focus. You came up with brilliant ideas, but you never worked hard enough to execute them."

Austin sighed and looked at the ground.

Beth continued. "Your attention span is getting shorter and shorter, and now there are errors showing up in your work. I think you're headed for a really bad place. In my opinion, you seem to be very distracted."

Austin had nothing to say.

Beth reached for her phone. "Listen, I want you to try this app."

She handed Austin her phone. He looked at the screen and saw the words: "Mindzone – Be Here Now."

"Download it and try it out. I really hope you can turn things around. I do have faith in you, Austin."

Beth left the room and Austin was alone. He felt depressed.

6.

ON A COOL SEPTEMBER evening, Shiv Patel walked with Tara and Malia and their dog along the San Francisco Marina. A fog had rolled in from the west and shrouded the Golden Gate Bridge. They strolled along the Marina past a row of docked luxury yachts.

Shiv loved to be with his daughters. However, as Google's CEO, he rarely had time for anything other than work. The girls were growing up too quickly; Malia was thirteen years old and Tara was nine. They attended private schools a few blocks away from their home. They were good kids, but lately Malia's interests had turned to boys and social media.

That evening, Shiv walked Teddy, a Golden Doodle with curly brown hair, with his daughters by his side. Tara skipped along, while Malia stared at her smartphone. They walked through the Marina and headed for the Palace of Fine Arts, a monumental structure originally constructed in 1915 for the Pacific Exposition. It looked like the Pantheon in Rome.

"Malia," Shiv asked. "How are things in school?"

Malia was busy texting on her smartphone.

"Malia!" Shiv said, grabbing the phone from her hand.

"Dad!" Malia yelled. "I was doing something!"

Shiv put her smartphone in his pocket. "Malia, I got a phone call from your school earlier today. They said you were involved in bullying behavior, and now I hear your grades are falling."

Malia stopped walking. "It wasn't my fault! Dad, I need my phone!"

Shiv stood his ground. "Every time I see you, you're on your smartphone. You are completely obsessed by it. I have no choice but to take away your phone for the rest of the month."

Malia stamped her foot. "Why are you doing this to me? It's not fair!"

Shiv stood firm. "I won't allow bad behavior. Once your grades improve, you'll get your phone back."

"What does the phone have to do with my grades?"

"Your phone *is* the problem! It's ruining your attention span!"

"How can you say that? Your company makes my phone. So it's all your fault, then!" After a few minutes, Malia quieted and then started to cry.

Shiv was sullen. As he and his daughters crossed the street, they walked past a homeless girl asking for change. She was in her early twenties and smelled like marijuana, and she had a small dog with her.

Tara frowned up at him. "Dad, why is that girl asking for money?"

Shiv hadn't noticed the homeless woman. He looked back and saw a girl with tattoos, dressed in ragged clothing. She was sitting on the ground with a cardboard sign that read: "Money for weed."

Shiv's initial impulse was to help the needy girl, but then he thought again and continued walking.

"She's a drug user," he said to his daughters. "That's what happens when you don't focus in school. You will end up just like her."

Malia was still upset. "Maybe your smartphone made her homeless, Dad."

Shiv grew upset. He was troubled by the state of today's youth. They were a distracted generation that had spent their entire lives on their smartphones, constantly obsessing about social media and not able to focus on anything for more than a few minutes. They faced a tough job market and insurmountable student loan debt.

Maybe Malia's right. My company's technology could be hurting young people. Maybe part of this is my fault.

The family was quiet as they walked around the Palace of Fine Arts. Shiv was deep in contemplation as he looked at the structure's spires and columns.

What can I possibly do to help the distracted state of America's youth? Surely as CEO of the world's largest technology company, there must be something I can do to help young people.

Shiv remembered the document he had written for the new Google employees – "Awaken the Power of Insight."

An idea struck him.

After walking around the Palace of Fine Arts, Shiv and his daughters went back to their sprawling home in the Marina district. Their butler greeted them. Shiv went to his study and grabbed his tablet.

"Anaya," Shiv said.

"Yes, Shiv," Anaya replied.

"I'd like to continue editing my document about insight."

Shiv re-read "Awaken the Power of Insight." Although he had written it for new Google employees, he knew he could also address it to America's youth. They desperately needed guidance and focus, and modern technology was driving them to the point of severe distraction. He felt compelled do something.

"Anaya, please create a new section."

"Okay, what would you like to call this section?"

"Distractions."

The title appeared on the screen. "In today's world, information is growing at an exponential rate. Every day, we are bombarded by a continuous stream of data from social media and other outlets. Why do some of us become so consumed with this information that it leads to a state of distraction? Is it possible to have a distracted mind and not be aware of it?"

He thought about it for a few minutes, contemplating with deep conviction. The answer became obvious.

"The key to answering these questions is awareness, an important mental ability that can illuminate the true condition of our minds. Awareness is a skill that can be nurtured and developed. Becoming aware is a key factor to our success and happiness. Awareness can be described as a state of awakened attention, where we can observe our thoughts and emotions without judgment."

Shiv paused and reflected.

I need to a way for people to understand awareness. For it to be useful, the method has to be simple and fast. It must be objective and standardized.

Shiv had an idea.

"To understand what is meant by awareness, please complete this five-minute awareness exercise."

Shiv dictated the instructions for a breathing exercise that he performed every morning after stretches and a cup of coffee.

Breathing exercise

Step 1 – Set a timer for five minutes, sit on a chair, and close your eyes.

Step 2 – Begin by taking a slow inhale and count for four seconds. Hold the breath for four seconds, and then exhale your breath for four seconds. This is one complete breath.

Step 3 – Count each breath at the end of each exhalation. Count these breaths from one to ten.

Step 4 – Once you have finished counting ten breaths, start over from the first breath. Continue counting breaths until the timer expires.

"This five-minute breathing exercise will give you awareness of your mind's state and help you become more mindful. As you take the long breaths, become aware of your breathing. Feel the air as it enters your nostrils, and feel your chest and abdomen rise and fall with each breath. Count each breath at the end of every exhalation. Be here, now, with your breathing.

"If you were not able to complete the exercise or if your breathing counts were interrupted several times through the exercise, then you may have a distracted mind. Ask yourself if you were able to focus on the present moment for an extended period. Were you interrupted by emotions, thoughts, or memories? Do you feel anxiety from unfinished tasks or plans? Imagine if you simply watched these interrupting thoughts without being affected by them in any way. By developing awareness of your distractions, it is possible for you to discover the true causes of your problems and achieve a state of peace and balance.

"This technique of watching your thoughts and distractions is awareness. It is a power you can develop that can transform a distracted mind into a focused one. Awareness is a wakeful attention you can use to peer into yourself and discover who you truly are.

"Everyone is capable of developing awareness and healing a distracted mind. The first step in the process is the realization that the mind is distracted. When this is appreciated, the process of healing the distracted mind can begin."

Shiv put down the tablet and walked to his living room, where he found his daughters watching television. Malia lay on a couch staring at a tablet computer. Shiv walked closer and saw she was video chatting with a boy.

"Malia!" Shiv yelled.

Malia jumped, the color draining from her face. Seeing his daughter afraid and vulnerable, Shiv felt remorseful. He went to hug her. He sat down with his daughters and watched television with them as they waited for dinner.

∞ ∞ ∞

A few hours later, Shiv showered and headed to bed. He had to wake up at 5 A.M. next morning and fly to Washington, D.C. for a Congressional hearing.

He was unable to sleep. He kept worrying about Malia. Her recent bad behavior began just as soon as she started using social media. He wished he had never given her a smartphone, but now it was too late. He knew many young people also suffered from the distractions of technology.

He grabbed his tablet.

"Anaya, open my document about insight."

"Opening."

Shiv looked through "Awaken the Power of Insight." He came across his figures depicting how insights develop in the mind.

What happens to insights in a distracted mind?

Shiv contemplated, rubbing his chin.

"Anaya, please cut and paste my first figure into this section."

The figure appeared. Shiv replaced the text and added lines, creating a new figure he called "A Model of Distractions."

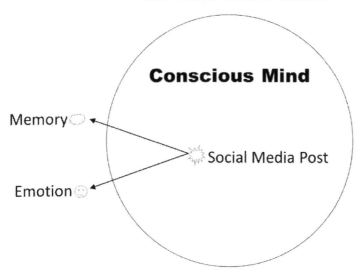

A Model of Distractions

"A distraction is anything that takes away our awareness of the present moment. There is nothing inherently wrong with a distraction. It is impossible to expect people to live free of all the distractions that are a feature of modern society. The problem arises when people engage emotionally with the distractions."

Shiv paused for a second. "For example, let's say we come across a social media post that triggers some emotion—a political tweet that makes us angry or a social media photo that makes us envious. The emotion from the distraction burrows into the subconscious mind and festers like a parasite. Later, the emotion returns to agitate us.

"The emotional engagement of information leads to repeated behaviors, and this is how distractions clog the mind. When we engage them, distractions diminish our attention span and make it difficult to be in the present moment. When the distractions transform into thought loops, we lose control of our minds."

Shiv drew another figure. Starting with "A Model of Distractions," he removed the lines and added curves, creating a new figure that he called "The Thought Loop."

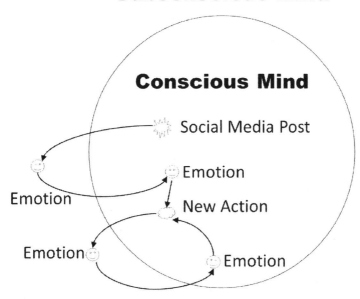

Subconscious Mind

Conscious Mind

Social Media Post

Emotion

Emotion

New Action

Emotion

Emotion

The Thought Loop

"In a thought loop, we experience recurring emotions from past events, trapping us in a cycle of distraction. For example, we remember an angry text message we received earlier in the day. Like a dust storm, the anger recurs and wreaks havoc. It triggers new actions—fights, road rage, inebriation. The process happens over and over – the thought loop.

"The emotional engagement with information leads to repeated patterns and behaviors, resulting in a distracted mind. The distracted person finds himself reliving past emotions and repeating past behaviors, incapable of being present in the now. Without awareness of this process, these thought loops continue endlessly and lead to a state of distraction."

Shiv stopped and reflected.

The Lost Generation—this is why they're suffering.

"Anaya, please copy and paste my last figure, but this time create 20 events and connect them with lines. Call it, 'A Model of the Distracted Mind.'"

"How about this?" Anaya asked. A new figure instantly appeared. Shiv modified it by adding new events, like tweets and text messages.

A Model of the Distracted Mind

Shiv looked at this model and saw in it the mental state of the world's youth. He knew he was on to something.

"Consider the massive amount of information we experience on a daily basis. Whenever we engage emotionally in new information, those emotions and memories result in thought loops. The process expands exponentially, and eventually the person is trapped in a distracted state. The mind is capable of becoming so distracted that it leads to a state of addiction, anxiety, or depression. The results are poor performance at school or work, sleep disturbances, a lack of confidence or ambition, and overall poor attention and shortsightedness.

"Now let's imagine what happens when someone with a distracted mind encounters a difficult challenge. His subconscious mind will solve the problem. However, because the distracted mind is bogged down in thought loops and unable to focus, the insight for that solution is never delivered to the conscious mind. The solution is ready, but the distracted mind is incapable of receiving the insight. Without the insight, the challenge is never solved. The distracted person has poor problem-solving skills, low innovation, and a lack of ideas. Ultimately, the distracted mind suffers from a lack of insight."

Shiv put down his tablet, but he was not happy with his writing.

This is too negative. I need to describe a way to heal the distracted mind. I have to end it on a positive note.

Shiv picked up the tablet. "It is possible to transform a distracted mind into a focused one. Healing the distracted mind will end the thought loops and bring a state of peace and focus. The mind becomes more insightful and innovative. The focused mind comes across the same bits of information as before, but it no longer reacts emotionally to the information. It is more disciplined and capable of recognizing distractions. As the distracted mind heals, the connection between the conscious and subconscious minds reopens, restoring insights to difficult problems.

"The first step in transforming a distracted mind is to develop an awareness of the underlying distracted condition. This means becoming aware of the emotions created in us when we experience our daily bits of information. It means becoming aware of the actions we take in response to past memories and emotions. Awareness is ultimately the antidote for a distracted mind. However, the process of developing awareness takes time and energy.

"During your five-minute breathing exercise, you may have been distracted by a thought or emotion that interrupted your counting. After you became aware of the distraction, you then continued the exercise. Although it lasted only a few seconds, that awareness of your distraction is the small seed of your rebirth. It is possible for this awareness to be nurtured and developed into a deep awareness that lasts throughout your day."

Shiv smiled and put down his tablet.

"Anaya, please prepare me for my morning flight."

"Okay, Shiv, I have set an alarm for 4 AM. Your flight to Washington, D.C., is on time."

7.

AUSTIN SANDERS WOKE UP in the middle of the night. It was 2:00 AM, and his ears were ringing. With a raging headache and a knot in the pit of his stomach, he lay in bed staring at the ceiling, unable to sleep. The memory of Beth and Karen recurred in his mind.

"We've decided to put you on a three-month probation period."

Austin rubbed his temples.

I can't believe Beth did this to me, all because of a few errors of code. What a bitch!

Austin grabbed his phone. "Molly, open Instagram."

He flipped through the photos and spotted his friend's Burning Man posts.

I've already seen all these.

"Molly, when's the next music festival?"

"The Dream State Festival is next weekend."

"Molly, can you order me the most popular e-cigarette?"

"E-cigarettes can cause cancer. Are you sure you want me to order one?"

Austin sighed. It seemed like nothing satisfied him anymore. The drugs, alcohol, and parties were catching up to him. He didn't sleep well at night, and sleeping pills weren't working. His doctor had prescribed him an anti-depressant, but it gave him dry mouth and constipation. Every solution he tried just gave him more problems.

Why can't I ever be satisfied? Any time I find something fun, I just want more of it.

In reality, Austin's distractions arose because of his new wealth. Google gave him a generous salary with benefits, stock options, and even an apartment rental subsidy. The more money he made, the more he desired. Lavish trips, clothes, video games – there were no limits. He could not stop himself from enjoying life.

Lying in bed unable to sleep, Austin remembered Beth's advice earlier that day. He grabbed his phone and downloaded Mindzone.

Beth said this app could turn things around. I doubt it.

He opened the app and the screen turned white. A bald gentleman appeared. "Welcome to Mindzone. This app will bring awareness and help heal a distracted mind. If you are suffering from anxiety, depression, or if you just feel unbalanced, it may be because of a distracted mind. Clearing your mind of distractions can give you peace and balance."

Austin rolled his eyes. He didn't have the patience to listen to a bald guy chattering about some bullshit.

"Molly, check the stock market futures."

A window popped up. Futures were in the red across the board, and it seemed like the market was set to crash. He scanned for more information and saw a headline: "European Union on verge of collapse."

He slammed his fists on the bed. "Goddamit!"

Maybe the bald guy on Mindzone was right. I have to clear my mind of distractions.

Frustrated, he flipped on Mindzone and continued listening.

"We will begin with an exercise," the bald man said. "It is a five-minute breathing exercise based on counting breaths. Sit upright, close your eyes, and take slow deep breaths."

Austin decided to follow the instructions. He sat upright on the edge of his bed and closed his eyes. His head throbbed, but he managed to sit through the pain for a few minutes.

With his eyes closed, Austin inhaled slowly for four seconds. He held his breath for another four seconds, and then slowly exhaled for four seconds.

This actually feels nice.

Slowing his breathing calmed him down. He counted each breath at the end of its exhalation, following the bald man's instructions. He tried to count his breaths from one to ten.

"Two...," Austin whispered to himself at the end of the second breath. A memory from Burning Man flooded his mind. It was the sculpture of a blue whale coming out of the desert sands, one of the trippiest exhibits at the festival. He was peaking on molly when he and friends looked up to see the massive metal whale.

Austin became aware that he had been distracted. He forgot how many breaths he had counted.

Was it two breaths or three?

Frustrated, he started the breathing exercise over with the first breath. This time, he counted three breaths before being interrupted by the memory of Karen Park. "Probation," she repeated in a stern tone.

Austin panicked.

What if I lose my job?

Another distraction, he realized. As soon as he counted a few breaths, another thought would enter his mind. With each interruption, he would have to start the breathing process over from the beginning.

The five-minute exercise ended, and the bald man returned. "During the breathing exercise, you may notice that you become easily distracted, and you may lose track of your counting. You may be in the middle of a breath when a sudden thought enters your mind, perhaps a memory, a reminder, or some other information. When you realize you've become distracted, simply continue the process of counting breaths. If you've forgotten the number of breaths, just start the process over with the first breath. You may find yourself interrupted several times during this breathing exercise. If this happens, do not become upset or judgmental in any way. Simply continue the exercise until it is completed."

Austin was intrigued. He decided to repeat the five-minute breathing exercise. This time he tried hard to maintain focus and count ten full breaths. He closed his eyes and inhaled, but like before, his counting was interrupted by a memory of Burning Man or Karen Park. Each interruption forced him to start counting over from the beginning. However, this time he didn't get angry or frustrated at himself; he simply made a note of the distraction, watching it slowly drift away.

Towards the end of the exercise, Austin became determined to stay focused. He managed to count to seven breaths before being distracted. He didn't judge himself after each distraction; instead, he just watched the distraction from a distance. His level of anger and frustration subsided, and his headache abated.

The timer went off – the five-minute exercise was over.

For once, I feel some peace.

For just a few minutes, he was able to forget his personal troubles and experience some calmness, something he hadn't felt in a long time. It was relaxing and almost euphoric.

Just then, Austin had an insight.

I'm overloaded with too much information! I need a break.

The bald man returned to the app. "Ask yourself what you truly want to achieve," he said. "Your dreams can be achieved if you have the right Mindzone. We will show you how to achieve your dreams."

Austin listened and asked himself what he truly wanted to achieve.

A new car would be nice. Maybe some solid returns on my stock portfolio?

Those were nice things to have, but he wanted to achieve something greater. He thought about it and the answer became obvious.

I want to be promoted. I want to move up to senior programmer.

The only path to promotion was a contribution to Project Bodi. He knew Bodi could be a breakthrough, and his demotion on the Bodi team was devastating. He wanted to get back on the team and lead it to success.

Maybe this Mindzone app can help me.

Little did he realize that he was to begin a journey that would transform his mind and lead to the launch of the most popular product of the decade.

PART 2

HEALING

8.

BETH SAT AT HER desk at Google Headquarters and tinkered with a prototype of the Bodi smartglasses. She placed them on her face.

"Cooper, what's the time?"

"It's 8:42 AM," the A.I. said through the speakers on the earpieces of the smartglasses.

"Cooper, switch to AR mode. Show me the time."

The time appeared in the top right corner. "8:42 AM."

The voice recognition seemed to work well, and Bodi's response time was excellent.

"Cooper, show me today's date."

The date appeared next to the time. "October 9, 2029."

It was two weeks after Quality Control's dismal assessment of Bodi's operating system, and Beth's team had made some minor progress during that time. Voice commands were now integrated into Bodi's software, but all Bodi could do in AR mode was to show the date and time. Major structural gaps still peppered its code.

Beth took off the smartglasses and assessed them. Though they looked like a pair of Ray-Ban sunglasses, inside the plastic frames of the smartglasses were the most state-of-the-art computer chips in the world. The processing power of Bodi's chips were faster than the supercomputer in 1997 or the laptop in 2017. Computing power continued to double every year, as predicted by Moore's law. Network speed was also rapidly progressing. Bodi could wirelessly live stream a video in 8K resolution without interruption.

"Cooper, send a text message to Sara."

"What would you like me to tell your assistant?"

"Ask her to come to my office."

Beth placed the Bodi glasses back on her face and peered around her office. The smartglasses were light and the frames were thin. Bodi was great so far in terms of style and comfort.

She tried to envision Bodi's Augmented Reality features.

What will it be like when it's fully functional?

She imagined seeing instant messages pop up in her field of view in real time.

How will you interact with pop-up messages? What if you're driving a vehicle and can't be disturbed? There are so many issues with Bodi's visual interface.

There was a knock on the door. "Come in," Beth called.

Sara walked in. "Hi, Beth. Did you want to see me?"

"Yes, come have a seat."

"Very cool glasses," Sara remarked to her boss. "I really like the Ray-ban style."

Beth laughed. "Style is the last thing on my mind. We have a long way to go to develop these smartglasses. I just hope we can finish in time to meet our deadline."

"Are we close to finishing it?"

Beth sighed. "Nowhere close. We have so many unknowns for this project that I'm starting to feel uneasy. There's a chance we won't succeed."

Sara gasped. "Oh no! Is the problem Augmented Reality?"

"Good memory, Sara. We are trying to program visual commands so that you control the glasses with your own eyes, which will make Bodi faster and more convenient than a smartphone. There's only one problem."

"What's that?"

"We've never created an operating system driven by visual commands."

Sara was silent. "So voice commands won't work?"

Beth nodded. "That's a good suggestion, but voice commands are too slow for the fast pace of modern communication. Wearable technology driven by voice would be cumbersome. They will never replace a smartphone."

Beth looked at her assistant and imagined Bodi's Augmented Reality. A small icon appeared over Sara's face. Beth clicked the icon and it turned into a small text tab. "Sara O'Brien, 650-555-2344, sobrien@google.com." Beth clicked on Sara's email address and dictated an email message to her.

"I have an idea," Sara said. "What if you design one cool Augmented Reality app, something that will get the public's interest? Then you can design other apps in a second-generation device."

"That's not a bad idea," Beth said, standing up and walking around her office. The printer paper for her copier was running low. In her imagination, she stared at the bar code on the packaging for the printer paper and up popped a small logo with the words: "Add to cart." She accepted the prompt and ordered three boxes of printer paper in just a few seconds.

Beth turned to Sara. "There's a fundamental problem with coding visual commands for Augmented Reality. How can we understand your intention?"

"How do you mean?"

Beth paused. "Let's say you're wearing the smartglasses and you stare at an object to learn more about it. How would Bodi know if you were interested in the object or if you were just mindlessly staring at it for no reason? What if you were having a conversation with someone and Bodi kept interrupting you with incoming messages and emails? There are so many challenges to programming Augmented Reality smartglasses operated by your eyes."

A phone rang and Sara got up. "I'll be right back."

Alone in her office, Beth developed serious doubts about Project Bodi. She wondered if taking on this project had been a mistake.

What if I can't deliver a working prototype? We have only four weeks remaining before the deadline!

Google executives were ruthless in their quest for perfection. Without a working device, they might take away her title or department privileges.

I've worked so hard to get here. It would be devastating if we fail!

Panic clutched at Beth's throat. Failure was becoming a real possibility. She had not felt this way in many years. The climb to success was turning into a steep slope.

What if my best days are behind me?

Knowing no good decisions were made in a state of anxiety, she tried to calm down before the emotions took over.

"Cooper, switch to VR mode."

The screen on her smartglasses darkened, and a white text box appeared. "What video will you like to see, Beth?"

Beth contemplated. "Play a meditation video."

Several dozen meditation videos appeared. Beth looked at her choices and recognized every video. Then she came across a new one.

"Play the Buddhist Monastery Meditation."

Immediately, Beth stood on stone steps overlooking a snow-capped mountain range. In front of her a massive mountain projected into the sky, its entire surface covered in snow. Clouds enshrouded the peak of the mountain. She felt the icy winds streaming down the mountain, and it sent shivers through her spine. The wind's power was tremendous.

This must be the Himalayas. I wonder if that's K-2.

Beth heard bells ringing in the distance. She looked to the left and right, and all she saw were more mountains covered in snow. It was a great mountain range extending far into the distance. She looked down at her feet and saw stone steps. She turned her head and followed the stone steps to a large structure built into the mountainside.

It was a monastery.

It looked like a fort. Its white walls projected high into the air, with defensive positions perched above to protect against invaders. Inside the perimeter were cloisters and an inner courtyard. The monastery walls were red, white, and yellow, a magnificent contrast to the snowy mountain peaks.

Three monks wearing red robes hung multi-colored flags near the structure's entrance. Each flag was a different color – red, yellow, white, green, and black. Beth regarded the monks with keen interest. She listened closely and heard bells in the distance.

The video started to move, and Beth was now walking towards the monastery. She approached the monks, busy with their flags. A large wooden door with engravings on its surface rose behind the monks. Before heading into the monastery, she turned around to get one last look at the mountains, taking in the beautiful view of the cloud-capped peaks.

Inside the monastery, Beth found a courtyard full of monks. A monk wearing red and yellow robes stood next to a large metal bell in the center of the courtyard. Every few seconds, the monk smashed the bell with a wooden ram, sending a loud clang into the surrounding mountainside. In front of the bell, seven rows of monks dressed in red robes sat in meditative posture. One of them led a chant of prayer in a deep voice that reverberated across the monastery. Above the sounds of the bell and the monk's prayer chant, the howling winds streamed down from the mountaintops.

Beth focused her attention on the sound of the bell. She closed her eyes and meditated. The monk in the front row chanted a mantra, and all the other monks joined the chant. Between the the bell and the mantra chant, there was a harmony of sounds. The music struck deep into her soul.

Beth sensed some anxiety trying to creep into her mind. It was worry over Project Bodi. The emotion disturbed her peace and took her away from the present moment. She thought about Augmented Reality coding. Instead of reacting to the anxiety, Beth just watched it. She labeled the emotion, observing it as an outsider. After a few seconds, the anxiety drifted away, and Beth returned to the monastery.

Beth was now in a state of awakened attention, fully aware of any thoughts or emotions that came into her consciousness. She decided to do a quick mental exercise. She closed her eyes and imagined a large triangle in front of her. She imagined her consciousness as an eye in the center of the triangle.

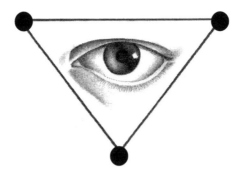

She visualized three words written around the triangle, one at each of the triangle's corners. The first word was "Compassion." She meditated on this word, thinking of actions related to compassion. She thought of empathy, kindness, and thoughtfulness, sending a message to her subconscious mind that compassion was an important trait to live by.

Beth then visualized the next point in the triangle, displaying the word "Devotion." She contemplated actions that it implied: resolve, strength, persistence. After meditating on "Devotion" for a few seconds, she then moved on the last point on the triangle, where she found the word "Innovation." She meditated on actions related to innovation: insight, knowledge, invention. Afterwards she visualized the entire triangle with all three words written at its points: "Compassion, Devotion, Innovation." She imagined herself sitting in the center of the triangle.

When Beth made decisions as Vice President and as head of her department, she tried to maintain a presence within the triangle encompassing these three qualities. She led with these principles at all times. She meditated on these three qualities every morning before going to work. In this way, she reinforced them as the primary drivers for her decision-making.

As Beth meditated in the monastery, there was a knock at the door.

Sara walked in. "Beth, that phone call was from Dr. Patel's office."

Beth removed her Bodi smartglasses and looked up to see her assistant. She sensed something was wrong.

"Is everything ok?" Beth asked.

"It's the Executive Committee," Sara said. "They are requesting an impromptu meeting for Friday. Related to Project Bodi."

"An impromptu meeting? But I just presented to the Committee last week!"

"I know," Sara consoled. "I told Dr. Patel's secretary that, and she said the Executive Committee wants another meeting because they're concerned about the 'lack of progress they're seeing from the Bodi team.' Those were her words."

Beth sighed. "This is ridiculous! I'm going to have to stand in front of the committee again and answer their impossible questions!"

"I'm sorry, Beth."

"We will need some key breakthroughs on Project Bodi soon. Otherwise this device is in jeopardy!"

Sara excused herself and left the office, and Beth was sullen. As she waved goodbye to her assistant, she was struck by a poster hanging on the wall. It was a map of the San Francisco Bay Area.

An idea came to her.

∞ ∞ ∞

Later that day, Beth held a meeting with the thirty-four members of her department. Her mood was somber.

"This is our second urgent team meeting this week," Beth said to start the meeting. "Bodi is in trouble."

Her team members shot worried glances at one another.

"The Executive Committee asked to see me again about our project. You can all imagine what this means. Without a working prototype by the end of the month, this program will be toast. We need major advancements on Project Bodi as soon as possible."

Beth's department members were quiet. Austin sat in the back row staring at the ground.

Beth commanded the room. "I want to go around and hear what everyone's working on. Please give me an update to your project."

She pointed to Paul, a lead programmer in the visual programming group.

Paul hesitated "... I've been working on the visual interface. I think I have a way to make visual commands select objects on the screen."

"How does it work?" Beth responded.

"Well, it's still a work in progress. Basically, when you stare at an object, an icon will appear. There will be options for search, communication, or whatever."

Beth shook her head. "No, Paul, we've discussed that option many times. It's impossible to program visual commands that way. Think about it. That will mean that everything you stare becomes an icon. It just won't work. You will have to come up with a better solution. Team, I will need every one of you to innovate when it comes to our challenge with visual commands. We need a revolutionary solution. The programmer who solves this will get a promotion."

Beth pointed to Jose, another lead programmer. "Jose, I have an idea for you. Our first Augmented Reality app should be Google Maps. It should be relatively easy to program Maps into a smartglasses format. I want you and your colleagues to work together on Google Maps for Bodi."

Jose gave a thumbs up. "No problema!"

A few laughs arose, the tension in the room dissipating.

Beth smiled. "Austin, what have you been working on?"

Austin seemed nervous, biting his fingernails and staring at the ground in fear. He started shaking and nervously fidgeting. Everyone looked at him.

"I've also been thinking about the visual commands," he said.

"And?" Beth asked.

"Well, I've got some ideas. But nothing is ready for prime time."

Beth rolled her eyes and moved on to the next programmer.

9.

"HEY COHEN, I'M NOT feeling well."

"What's the matter, Austin?"

Austin and Cohen were at the patio of a nightclub in San Francisco. It was two weeks since Austin's probationary meeting with Karen Park.

Austin rubbed his belly. "Something's off. I'm not feeling right."

"You were fine an hour ago," Cohen said. "Look at all these Snaps we've taken already!"

Austin was high and drunk. The music was somehow not as euphoric as usual. He blamed it on the DJ. Austin had spent the night talking to people and smoking their cigarettes. He kept chasing euphoria, but it was elusive; the music, smoking, and partying didn't give him any lift this time. Something was wrong.

Maybe I took a bad batch of molly. Or maybe I shouldn't have mixed molly and alcohol.

In the two weeks since his meeting with Karen Park, Austin was trying his best to heal his distracted mind. It was a difficult process. He had appreciated the cluttered mess in his mind, but he didn't know how to fix it. He could not sleep well and often woke up in the middle of the night with nightmares, not able to fall back asleep for hours. In the mornings, he was tired and restless.

Austin lit a cigarette in the club's outdoor patio. "I think there's something wrong with me."

Cohen shook his head. "Yeah man, you're not your usual self. You keep going back and forth from the stage to the patio. Seems like something's bothering you."

Austin threw his cigarette on the ground. "It just feels like nothing can satisfy me. It's hard to describe. It feels like I'm in purgatory."

"Let me get you a Ryde." A Ryde was the latest thing – a driverless taxi that was cheaper than a bus.

The Ryde arrived in a few seconds and Austin crawled in, vomiting on the way home.

The next morning, Austin had a raging headache and continued vomiting. He sat on the bathroom floor hugging the cold toilet. Every time he tried to stand, a wave of nausea forced him to sit back down. His phone constantly buzzed with text messages, snaps, and tweets.

Why did I drink so much?

Austin sat on his bathroom floor with vomit hanging from his mouth. His ears were ringing and his head throbbed. He glanced at the notifications from his phone and it made him feel sicker.

"Molly, open my Mindzone app."

The bald man appeared. "Today is a new day for peace and progress. We will start today with a five-minute listening exercise. Please sit upright on a chair or on the floor with your back fully supported."

Austin sat on a bath rug and supported his back against the wall.

"Start with four slow deep breaths," the bald man continued. "Be aware of each breath as it enters and exits your nostrils."

Austin took in a deep breath. He felt the cold air entering his nostrils and felt his chest expand, then let the warm air exit his nostrils. It actually felt pleasant. He took another breath and then was interrupted by a thought about his Tesla stock position. He grabbed his phone to check on Tesla's stock value. After a few seconds, he realized that he had been distracted away from the Mindzone exercise.

Choking back his frustration, he returned to the exercise.

"Close your eyes," the bald man continued. Austin continued breathing deeply and then slowly closed his eyes. "For this exercise, focus on the sounds around you. Become aware of all the sounds in your environment. Listen to each sound for a few seconds. Be present in this moment."

Austin became aware of the present moment and listened for any sounds. He heard a lawn mower in the distance, some birds in the trees nearby, a car driving by his apartment. He listened more closely and concentrated. He heard the sounds of a busy freeway in the far distance and an airplane high above. He heard lawn sprinklers. He listened to each sound for several seconds, noting its quality and length.

For five minutes, Austin listened to each sound coming from outside his bathroom window. Surprisingly, he wasn't distracted during the listening exercise. He had even received a Tweet notification and had just listened to its sound without responding to it. It was a first for him.

The five-minute exercise ended.

Finally some peace....

It was euphoric. The nausea went away and his headache improved. He felt like he was finally free. No medicine or drug had ever given him such peace.

How can I make this peace last the entire day?

As soon as the exercise ended, the distractions came right back. Social media notifications and text messages flooded his phone. He remembered his stock positions and went to check some stock quotes, and then he checked Twitter and Snapchat. The peace he had experienced was only transient.

Austin stared at his phone. An insight came to him.

This is the source of my problems! My peace went away just as soon as I picked up my phone.

He threw his phone onto the floor.

How am I supposed to get rid of these distractions? The world is racing at a million miles an hour and I'm along for the ride. Peace is impossible!

Austin's phone beeped with a new notification. "Molly, who just texted me?"

"It's Cohen. He says 'Guess what? W&W are coming to town!'"

W&W were hardcore electronic music DJs, and their shows were intense.

The text message was an instant trigger, and Austin immediately craved another night of drugs and alcohol. This time he had mixed feelings. He thought about the club in San Francisco the night before.

What a depressing night.

The molly should have made for a fantastic night, but it hadn't been fun at all. The euphoria only lasted an hour, and then he ended up chasing it for the rest of the night. He didn't want to repeat the experience anytime soon.

The urge for drugs took over Austin's decision-making. He craved some drug-induced euphoria, but he didn't want another night of molly and electronic music. He decided to take a break from the molly.

"I'll pass," Austin texted back to Cohen. "Got other plans."

Austin passed on the W&W concert, but he still had the urge to do drugs. The trigger from his friend's text was so strong that it set off a thought loop of desire in Austin's mind. He wanted to do drugs, but perhaps in a more relaxed environment. He did love the peace and tranquility he felt after a Mindzone mindfulness exercise.

What if I combine drugs and meditation? That could be far out.

He thought about planning a camping trip and bringing some psychedelics, maybe some peyote in the desert. Or maybe a trip to the beach with friends and some LSD. Soon his mind was fixated on doing drugs, and it became the central focus of his desire.

Just then, Austin had another insight.

Drugs are taking over my life. Just a few minutes ago, I was in a state of peace after a Mindzone exercise. Just one text message and all that peace evaporated!

Austin focused his awareness on the cravings. He watched the feelings of desire, listening to them as he had listened to the sounds of the lawnmower and water sprinklers. He applied the same techniques from the Mindzone app to the thoughts of desire entering his mind.

I'm using drugs to escape.

It was an insight that most drug users never receive.

What am I escaping?

He thought about his work life and his personal life.

Am I happy with my life?

He had a great group of friends, but somehow he never found a girlfriend. He had not called his parents for several months. His situation at work was continuing to deteriorate. Austin looked at his own life from high above, and he did not like what he saw. Somehow, he would have to change.

∞ ∞ ∞

Austin managed to get himself together and drive to work. He took some ibuprofen for his headache and it helped somewhat, but he could not focus. At work, he tried to write some code for Project Bodi. After three hours of work, he managed to enter only five lines of code. His concentration was poor, and every few minutes there was another text, Snapchat, or Tweet notification on his phone.

Austin stared at his computer.

I just can't focus. What if I do a Mindzone exercise to help me focus?

The mindfulness exercise would bring some peace, but it seemed to be temporary. After the exercise was over, he would be right back to his distracted state.

I need a peace that lasts. How do I get that? Is there a way to get some peace and freedom that lasts longer than five minutes?

"Molly, how do I get long term peace?"

"I'm afraid I can't give you that."

Austin rolled his eyes. "Molly, I like the peace I feel after a Mindzone exercise. How can I make it last?"

"Try a longer Mindzone exercise."

What a bitch!

Out of nowhere, a craving for drugs entered Austin's mind. It was a memory from Burning Man—the blue whale sculpture springing out of the desert sands. The memory of the sculpture made him want to do some drugs.

"Molly, search for drugs and meditation."

"A web search turns up this book."

Austin looked at the search result with great interest. It was a link to a book called "The Psychedelic Experience: A Manual Based on the Tibetan Book the Dead," written in 1964 by Timothy Leary and others. The book helped launch the psychedelic movement of the 1960's. It described how the proper use of psychedelic drugs, such as LSD, magic mushrooms, or peyote, could lead to a state of Nirvana. Austin didn't know what Nirvana referred to, but it sounded like something he needed in his life. He started to read the book.

"A psychedelic experience is a journey to new realms of consciousness," the book began. "The scope and content of the experience is limitless, but its characteristic features are the transcendence of verbal concepts, of space-time dimensions, and of the ego or identity."

Austin thought about his trip to Burning Man when he and his friends had done LSD for the first time.

I don't remember any transcendence of space-time dimensions or ego. It was just a really fun weekend with lots of cool music and great Snaps.

Austin continued reading. "Such experiences of enlarged consciousness can occur in a variety of ways: Sensory deprivation, yoga exercises, disciplined meditation, religious or aesthetic ecstasies, or spontaneously. Most recently they have become available to anyone through the ingestion of psychedelic drugs such as LSD, psilocybin, mescaline, DMT, etc."

Austin jaw dropped.

Psychedelic drugs can give me the same peace and enlightenment as mindfulness meditation?

The book described how set and setting were key to reaching the enlightened state during a psychedelic trip. It drew parallels between a psychedelic experience and the experience of death and rebirth according to the Tibetan Book of the Dead, an ancient text of Buddhist philosophy.

Austin read the book with deep interest. He learned about the different stages of the psychedelic trip. "The first sign is the glimpsing of the Clear Light of Reality," the book wrote of the drug experience. "In this state, realization of what mystics call the 'Ultimate Truth' is possible.... Liberation is the nervous system devoid of mental-conceptual activity."

The book described the process of ego loss, wherein the individual's ego and routine mental processes were temporarily halted, leading to a state of infinite awareness. All of this was possible with the ingestion of LSD, peyote, or magic mushrooms, according to the book. Setting the expectations beforehand was key to unlocking the experience.

Austin wanted to experience this for himself. "Molly, does LSD lead to Nirvana?"

"According to the Dalai Lama, drugs are part of the egoistic desire that leads to a continuous state of suffering. Liberation from desire and attainment of Nirvana is only possible only by cessation of desire."

"What the hell are you talking about, Molly?"

Austin rolled his eyes and went back to the "Psychedelic Experience." The book recommended using high doses of LSD or peyote to achieve the state of ego loss liberation. The doses were much higher than what he had tried at Burning Man.

Austin was intrigued.

What if I take LSD and liberate myself from these constant distractions? What if instead of doing these drugs at a music festival, I take it and meditate for the day....

He glanced at the book. "Set and setting are keys to unlocking the psychedelic experience."

Maybe I can reach a state of enlightenment.

Austin finished the entire book in one sitting, and he grew extremely excited. He decided to try it out the following day.

∞ ∞ ∞

Austin awoke early on Saturday morning and walked to his fridge to check on his drug supply. He still had seven tabs of LSD from Burning Man. He had barely felt the single LSD tab at the festival, so he assumed the tabs were low quality.

Austin decided to take five tabs, a dose of 500 micrograms. This was the dose of LSD recommended in the book.

Without any hesitation, he placed the LSD blotters under his tongue and waited. He walked to his backyard and sat in a chair. Anxiety set in.

Should I have taken so many? It's only my second trip.

Within a few minutes, his stomach squirmed and his heart raced. He felt a mild wave of nausea, a familiar feeling from his previous LSD experience. However, that time the nausea started about an hour after taking the dose. This time it came on in just a few minutes.

Austin grew nervous, wondering if Beth or Karen would somehow find him. Feeling his anxiety increasing, he opened the Mindzone App and began a mindfulness exercise, focusing on his breaths. His mind raced and his heart pounded in his chest. He closed his eyes and meditated. Colors appeared.

Austin looked at a garden in the distance. The red and purple colors of the flowers jumped out like the pages of a pop-up book. He had never seen such vibrant colors before. It felt like he was seeing the real beauty of the world for the first time.

Every few seconds, there were sounds coming from Austin's phone. There were notifications, instant messages, tweets, and emails. For once, Austin didn't care to check his phone. He marveled at the raw beauty and vastness of the blue sky. It was such a deep, heavenly blue. The clouds were delicate and infinitely complex. And the light coming from the sun was brighter than he ever remembered.

Why am I never aware of the infinite beauty of the world?

Free of distractions, Austin was able to see the world as it truly is – a marvelous, heavenly place full of life.

Austin looked down at the ground and saw small shapes in the concrete. There were hexagons, octagons, and other complex shapes in the ground. The shapes moved in spirals beneath him. It looked like a galaxy of stars right there in the concrete. He was peering into the geometrical organization embedded deep in his cerebral cortex.

He looked up at a tree and saw the same complex geometry. It felt like he was seeing the true nature of the tree for the first time. He gazed at the fine detail of the tree trunk and its branches and leaves. It was a living being right there in his backyard.

Austin peered closer and it seemed like the tree was breathing. Air flowed into the tree's trunk, its windpipe. The air went from the tree's trunk into its branches and leaves. Every few seconds, the tree took in a deep breath and then exhaled it. The tree was a giant pair of lungs. He saw that his own lungs had the same structure as the tree. The tree's trunk, branches, and leaves looked very much like his own lungs with airways, bronchi, and alveoli. They were both living organisms designed with a similar structure. Austin felt at one with the tree. They both originated from a common ancestor a very long time ago.

The LSD fully kicked in. Austin looked up at the heavens and his mom's face appeared in the blue sky. He felt a deep sense of love for his mom. His anxiety disappeared, replaced by love. He wondered why he hadn't called his mother in so long. He had been so busy at work that he had forgotten to say hello to her.

Mom, I love you.

Then his dad's face appeared in the sky next to his mom's face.

Dad, I miss you.

Austin closed his eyes and felt a warm breeze coddling him. He opened his eyes, and above his mom and dad, he saw the faces of his grandparents, whom he loved so dearly. Above them appeared their parent's faces, and above their faces appeared more faces. A tree of life formed in the sky. It went back for hundreds of generations, and soon there were thousands of people in the sky above him.

Austin had an epiphany.

These are my ancestors, and they're going back further and further in time to the beginning of the universe.

The universe was a living, breathing organism with a deep consciousness. This was the essence of the universe, and it existed on a far grander scale than he had ever imagined.

At that moment, Austin felt truly at one with the universe. He was a link in a chain of life that went back in time for billions of years. He felt a deep sense of love and security. For thousands of generations, his ancestors had experienced the same worries and doubts that now troubled him.

There's no reason to worry. Everything will fall into place as it always has.

An unseen dimension of the universe appeared before him, revealing the commonality of life and the essence of being. Austin's awareness of the universe gave him an infinite peace and inner harmony. His awareness expanded and reached the level of cosmic consciousness, its highest possible form in the universe.

As Austin stared at the sky, the light from the sun turned brighter. The sun grew larger and larger in front of him. Every second it expanded a few inches.

What is going on?

The sun kept getting larger, replacing the clouds and blue sky with pure light. Then everything turned to light.

In one instant, Austin lost all sense of time, vision, hearing, feeling, and smell. He was experiencing ego death. He lost all awareness of the world around him for one brief moment of time. He vanished from existence.

As instantly as Austin exited the universe, he just as quickly returned.

He first became of aware of time passing in microseconds. Each microsecond of time had its own individual quality, like the teeth of a long comb. He didn't think it was possible to be aware of time in microseconds, and here he was experiencing it for the first time. Time then sped up, and he became aware of it passing in milliseconds, and then in seconds.

Austin's ego had simply vanished. His consciousness had vaporized out of existence, and now it was returning in a different form. The first emotion he became aware was an overwhelming feeling of trauma, as a baby feels when he exits the womb and enters the strange new environment of the world. The trauma was excruciatingly painful. Austin was re-entering the world, as if for the first time.

After a few seconds, the feeling of trauma subsided, and Austin's awareness slowly came back into its full form. He looked around at the trees and flowers. Every living being radiated. Even the ants on the ground were glowing with life. His consciousness had merged with the universe. There was no difference between him and all the life forms around him.

He opened his eyes and saw a bird showering a pink vapor trail. It merged with the shimmering green of the plants around him. Wind chimes turned into vibrating rainbows as they floated through the air.

Austin immersed himself in the present moment, merging with the sounds, actions, and living beings in his environment. He closed his eyes and felt a multidimensional being morphing from mass to energy.

God, is that You?

God and the Universe, energy and matter, being and consciousness. The mystery of the universe revealed itself.

Suddenly a harsh ringing billowed through the air, and the sky turned grey. It came from his smartphone, a social media notification. Austin looked at his phone and it transformed into a black hole, sucking in light and energy. Without his ego, Austin was unarmed against the dark forces of his addictions.

A translucent demon surrounded Austin, trembling the ground as it spoke. "I have some molly for you. It's gonna be a fun night."

A sharp pain struck Austin's back. He looked up at the sky and his family disappeared. The sky turned black, and a giant metal wheel appeared.

"Get on the wheel, Austin. You are going to be rich and famous. All the drugs you want. It's infinite."

The wheel started spinning.

"Get on the wheel and start running, Austin. You'll get to your destination soon enough."

Austin panicked and ran into the house. He became aware that he had ingested a large quantity of psychedelic drugs.

What have I done to myself?

Beth appeared in the hallway. "I'm ending your probation. You're fired as of this moment."

Austin ran into his bedroom, slamming the door behind him. He saw numbers on his computer screen. He looked closer and his bank account read "$0.00."

Panic set in.

I lost my job and now I have no money! How am I going to pay the rent?

He turned and his parents appeared in front of him. "What are you doing, son? Are you out of your mind?"

Austin ran into the hallway and the dean of his university appeared. "We need our degree back."

He ran the other way and saw his high school principal. "We are taking your honors awards away."

I'm losing everything I've worked so hard for!

He heard the doorbell ring. Someone was at the door.

It must be Beth!

He ran into the bathroom and shut the door behind him, but the doorbell kept ringing. It grew louder. Beth wanted to see him immediately.

I can't escape! I have to end my life right now.

Austin's heart raced madly. He broke down.

"Help, anyone!" he shouted at the top of his lungs.

What will be the easiest way to end it?

He imagined himself lying dead on the floor.

Who will find my body?

The thoughts kept racing in his mind. He needed help immediately. At the top of his lungs he shouted, "Dial 9-1-1!"

Austin's Google Home speaker began to make a phone call.

"9-1-1 operator," the voice said.

"Please help!" Austin yelled. "My life is over!"

Austin paced around the bathroom crying deliriously.

"Sir, tell me what's happening," the operator said.

"Beth is here for me! This is the end of the road. I have to end my life right now!"

An ambulance siren blared in the distance. Austin looked out the window in confusion. The sirens grew louder.

They are coming for me!

Austin felt an overwhelming relief when he realized the ambulance was for him. It threw him back into reality.

Help is coming!

"Thank you!" Austin yelled to the 911 operator. "Thank you so much!"

Austin sat and cried on the floor. There was a knock on the door.

Austin got up and ran to the front door, where he saw three tall paramedics wearing jumpsuits.

They were frightened to see him. Austin's pupils were extremely dilated and he was disheveled. He looked like a vagabond.

"I'm so happy to see you," Austin told them.

The paramedics kept their distance for a few seconds. Sensing Austin was not a threat, they instructed him to sit down on the ground. They took off his T-shirt and then placed small ECG sticky pads on his upper body.

"Sinus normal rhythm, tachycardia," one of the paramedics said aloud.

"Normal O2 sat," another paramedic said.

The paramedic removed the ECG pads. "Sir, what's been happening?"

Austin responded without hesitation. "I took some LSD and had a bad trip. I was really going to hurt myself."

One paramedic shone a flashlight in Austin's eyes. "Pupils extremely dilated, not responsive to light. Heart rate 120. Breath rapid and shallow."

"Sir, is there someone here with you?" a paramedic asked.

Austin felt a deep sense of shame. "No, I'm here alone," he said, his mind jumbled. "I saw the meaning of the universe just now. It all makes sense."

The paramedics chuckled. They looked at Austin's body for any signs of injury or abuse and found nothing.

"So, what's the meaning of the universe?" one of the paramedics asked him.

Austin could not find the words. "Well..." He tried to gather his thoughts. "Everything we are doing at this moment has been done for thousands of generations. It's so hard to describe.... There's no reason to worry about stuff. Everything will all come together on its own."

"Sir, we're gonna take you to the hospital," one of the paramedics replied. "We'll need to keep an eye on you until you stabilize."

Austin put his head down and cried. He was deeply ashamed of his actions. He wanted to apologize to his parents and Beth.

"I'm so sorry, guys. I'm sorry for wasting your time."

"It's not a waste of time, sir. It's our job. We're glad to be here for you."

After a while, Austin stopped crying and walked to the ambulance.

10.

ON A FOGGY SATURDAY afternoon, Shiv and Malia jogged through the Presidio District of San Francisco. The Presidio was a World War II military base that was undergoing a Renaissance; it had recently become a hotbed for tech start-up companies.

Shiv had modified his work schedule to allow more time with his daughters, and there were positive results almost immediately. In the few weeks since her dad took away her cell phone, Malia rebounded at school. She engaged with people and no longer fought with Tara.

Shiv and Malia stopped jogging to take a rest when they saw a homeless girl sitting on the sidewalk ahead. It was the same homeless girl as before. She had a small dog with her and a cardboard sign: "Money for Weed."

Malia pointed at the girl. "Dad, she's back."

Shiv looked at the homeless girl with concern. "Malia, it's not nice to point."

They walked past the homeless girl, and Shiv felt compelled to say something. "Do you need help?"

"No," the girl replied. She had several lip rings, and tattoos on her arms. "I just need a dollar."

Shiv reached into his pocket. "I'd like to help you. But I won't give you money if you'll use it for drugs."

The homeless girl rolled her eyes. "Then I don't need your money."

Shiv's eyebrows rose. He and Malia continued walking home, and they soon left the Presidio district and entered the Marina.

"I can't believe she said that to me," Shiv remarked to Malia.

"I can. There are girls in my school just like her."

"Really? How do you mean?"

"They use drugs and they ditch school."

Shiv grew upset. "Well, this is why I always said that marijuana should not be legalized. Marijuana is a gateway drug that leads to other drug addictions. And I even read a study that marijuana use in teenagers leads to schizophrenia."

Malia stopped walking. "Well, what do you expect, Dad? Things are hard for my generation. Do you know how much it costs to go to college now? Most of my friends won't go to college because they can't afford it. Do you know what they call my generation?"

Shiv shook his head. "What?"

"The Lost Generation."

Shiv put his arm around Malia. "I didn't know that." He grew silent.

We are failing our children.

As he and his daughter jogged back home, he felt compelled to do something for America's youth. As CEO of the world's largest company, he had the power to make a difference.

There must be something I can do to help young people.

After they arrived back home, Shiv walked to his study and grabbed his tablet computer.

I must send a message to the so-called Lost Generation. To warn them of the dangers of addiction, a core problem for them.

"Anaya, I'd like to continue editing my document about insight," Shiv said.

The document appeared on the tablet.

"Anaya, create a new section called 'Addiction.'"

The sub-heading appeared.

"In today's world, drug use is a major cause of crime, imprisonment, and early mortality. The primary driver of drug use is addiction, but drug use isn't the only form of addiction. Another major addiction is technology, which can also take away someone's freedom and well-being."

Shiv looked at the document.

Somehow I have to reach the distracted youth.

"The human mind operates in a way that allows it to become addicted to any activity. And the nature of addictions is such that we lack awareness of their existence. In the social media age, the pursuit of information has become an addiction, one that has changed billions of lives. It is important to understand how addictions arise because the process of addiction is the same, regardless of the addictive behavior.

"There are the obvious addictions: cigarettes, alcohol, and opiates. The addictions exist as thought loops in the mind. An addiction is a cycle of emotion, behavior, and reward that drives itself perpetually. For example, cigarette smoking triggers a desirable emotion, euphoria, in the conscious mind. The euphoria and the memories of the smoking are transferred to the subconscious mind. Sometime later, perhaps during a challenging moment in our day, the memory of the euphoria returns to the conscious mind, creating an intense craving. Before long the addiction must be satisfied again."

Shiv reached for a glass of water. "Anaya, can you copy and paste my previous figure about the Thought Loop."

The figure appeared. With some modifications, Shiv created a new figure he called, "A Model of Addiction."

Subconscious Mind

Conscious Mind

Activity

Craving

Reward

Addictive Activity

Reward

Craving

A Model of Addiction

"In the analogy of the conscious mind as a circle, an addiction has a structure similar to the thought loop. The 'addictive activity' is anything that triggers a desirable emotion, such as cigarette smoking, shopping, or tweeting. We engage in this activity in our conscious mind and experience an emotional reward, such as euphoria, and that memory is stored in our subconscious mind. Some time later, the memory of the reward comes back into our conscious mind, creating an intense craving. In our moment of stress, we desperately need that emotional reward to cope with the stress. The activity, reward, and craving create a cycle of addiction. Ironically, it is the desire itself that starts the cycle of addiction. The cause of our suffering is desire itself."

Shiv paused and reflected. He remembered Malia's earlier troubles at school.

She rebounded soon after I took away her smartphone.

He continued to dictate.

"There are many addictions in modern society that are subtle and seem less harmful. These addictions may be driving our decision-making without our awareness. Our smartphones have become a central addiction that runs our daily lives, from the moment we awaken to the time we sleep. Every few minutes, we may be compelled to check our social media feeds, tweets, or emails. Checking Snapchat, Wired, or Instagram feeds constantly throughout the day is an addictive behavior that can lead to dissatisfaction, anxiety, or even depression.

"For any addiction, the process begins when a behavior triggers a desirable emotion or reward. The first time we used Instagram or Snapchat, we experienced intense feelings of joy and laughter. It was wonderful to check our social media feeds and interact with our friends and family. We checked our social media more often in search of that same joy and laughter. Over time, those rewards diminish, but we continue to engage in the behavior. We may soon find ourselves checking social media constantly throughout the day for no real purpose other than to satisfy our thought loop. We may not even be aware of this addictive behavior, and yet it may be a source of our mental health problems. It may be the reason for our sleep problems, anxiety, or depression, and we may not even be aware of it.

"A distraction becomes an addiction when it affects our judgment, decision-making, and daily functioning. The addiction slowly takes over our lives. Initially, the effects of the addiction may be subtle or even unrecognizable. As we continue to engage in the addictive activity and further relinquish our self-control, the addiction comes to dominate our lives. The addictive activity, once a source of happiness, now no longer satisfies us. We further engage in the addiction looking for the reward, and our mental imbalance just keeps growing over time. Soon we find ourselves hurtling down a road of misery, and we aren't even aware that these addictions are the cause of our suffering."

Shiv stopped and looked at the document. The last word of the document struck him: "suffering." He thought about the word "suffering" and it reminded him of the four Noble Truths of Buddhism.

What I wrote reflects the first two Noble Truths of Buddhism.

Shiv paused. He remembered the homeless girl and the way she rejected his offer to help.

I need to offer my readers a method for improving their lives. I need to convey the third Noble Truth.

An idea came to him.

"How can we free ourselves from a state of suffering? Once we become aware of our addictions, how can we cure them? How do we achieve liberation?"

Shiv looked up and saw the Golden Gate Bridge from his study. He smiled as it all came together.

"The solution lies in just one word: awareness. The same awareness that allowed us to identify the addiction and its effects in our lives is the same power we can use to end that addiction and heal our minds. Awareness is an amazing mental quality that all human beings can develop. It is capable of ending thought loops and undesirable addictions. It can liberate us from suffering and put an end to our anxiety and depression. Becoming aware can awaken our inner spirits, give us self-confidence, and make us truly happy in our core. It can improve the communication between our conscious and subconscious, transforming a distracted mind into a focused mind and taking us to our full potential.

"Awareness is a state of awakened attention. Imagine you are at a museum standing in front of a Picasso painting. You can view the painting by reading its title on the wall plaque and then briefly scanning the artwork. In this way, you notice the painting, but you are not truly aware of it. Awakened attention means really looking at the painting to understand its message. It means deciphering the true meaning of the artwork and the intention of the artist. In this way, you can develop awareness of the painting. It takes energy and curiosity to develop awareness. Awareness requires a state of wakefulness.

"Becoming aware of yourself means applying the quality of awakened attention to your own thoughts and emotions. Just as you analyzed the Picasso painting to discover its meaning, you can analyze your own thoughts and emotions and discover who you truly are. It is not enough to simply notice your thoughts. It requires awakened attention, and this takes practice and patience. When you become truly aware of yourself, you will identify the sources of your problems and realize what you need to do to improve your well-being."

Shiv smiled and remembered the words of his father, who was disciplined and nurturing. His father had taught him a meditation involving a process called "noting." Even to the present day, Shiv practiced his father's noting meditation. With inspiration from the memory of this father, Shiv designed the following exercise on his tablet computer with Anaya's assistance.

Noting exercise
    Step 1 – Set a timer for five minutes and sit on a chair (or on the floor with your back supported).
    Step 2 – Begin by taking four slow breaths, and then gently close your eyes.

Step 3 – Mentally scan your body starting from your head and slowly moving down to your toes. Notice any sensations or discomforts in each part of your body.

Step 4 – Anytime you are interrupted by a thought or emotion, become aware of it. Note the thought or emotion without any judgment. Label it as a "thought" or an "emotion" and give it a quality ("positive" or "negative"). Watch the thought or emotion until it disappears.

Step 5 – Continue to mentally scan your body until the timer expires.

After jotting down the exercise, Shiv continued dictating.

"This exercise will demonstrate awareness of thoughts. Just as before, spend a few minutes taking a few deep breaths and entering the present moment. Be here now. During the exercise, you may be interrupted by thoughts, memories, emotions, and desires. The key to the exercise is to become aware of the interrupting thought and to watch the thought carefully. Note the thought, give it a name, allow it to disappear, and then to return to the exercise. The act of returning to the present moment is how awareness develops over time. With repeated practice, you will become more aware of your thoughts, and this will gradually lead to deeper insight into your own problems and motivations.

"An important key to the exercise is repetition. Repeat mindfulness exercises every morning and think of them as stretching exercises for your mind. Over time, you will find that distractions and addictions will have less control of your life. Change requires patience. The development of awareness will transform a distracted mind into a focused one. This will translate into more insight and success. Listening to yourself will awaken your inner spirits. Awareness is the solution for the liberation of the distracted mind."

Shiv stopped dictating and looked at his document.

"Anaya, copy and paste my last figure here. Also add an image of an eye inside the circle."

Shiv modified the figure some more, creating a new figure he called "A Model of Awareness."

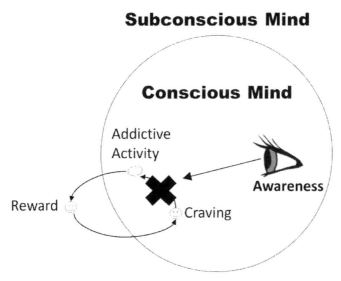

Subconscious Mind
Conscious Mind

A Model of Awareness

"In the analogy of our mind as a circle, awareness is a third eye that will peer into our thoughts and emotions. When we practice mindfulness, we open our third eye and focus it on our emotions and thoughts. We use our third eye to become aware of our desires and addictions; when we see a craving enter our mind, we can watch it with awakened attention. Just like we analyzed the Picasso painting in the museum, we can become mindful of the craving and observe its effects on our lives. As soon we become aware of our addictions, the source of our problems will become obvious.

"Addictions are deathly afraid of awareness, just as darkness hates the light. When we foster the third eye of awareness, its power grows. Nurtured and cultivated, it will grow stronger than our addictions. When it is fully open, the eye of awareness will block the ability of cravings to trigger addictive behaviors. The cycle of addiction will stop. Our third eye will make us fully realize the consequences of our addiction, so that we can stop the sequence leading to the addiction. When we realize the consequence, we will not start the sequence."

There was a knock at the door. "Dr. Patel, dinner is ready."

"Coming."

"Of course, there are addictions that can't be cured by meditation alone. Cigarettes, alcohol, and opiates have devastating withdrawal symptoms that trap you into a prison of abuse. There is a new FDA-approved drug, Provega, that cures heroin addiction. Interestingly, this drug works by expanding the mind's awareness just as meditation does.

"The power of awareness has been known to Sufis, Buddhists, and other ancient religions. This knowledge has been available for thousands of years. In modern society, the acceleration of information and technology is creating a world of perpetual distraction and addiction. There is a strong need to return to the wisdom of ancient teachings. To heal our distracted minds, we must return to the tools of long ago. We must return to a state of awakened attention and develop the power of awareness, so that we can rediscover our universe and ourselves."

Shiv put down his tablet and headed for dinner. Along the way, his phone pinged with a new meeting notification from Ed Koch's office: "Impromptu Meeting to discuss Project Bodi."

Shiv grimaced.

Ed wants to take Bodi down. I can't let this project fail.

11.

AUSTIN WAS STILL HIGH on LSD when he was wheeled into the Emergency Room at Kaiser Permanente Hospital in Palo Alto. Shirtless and disheveled, he lay on a gurney with his head in his hands. He had cried during the ambulance ride to the hospital.

What have I done to myself?

The paramedics rolled him into the triage room. There Austin found himself amid three other patients: an unconscious homeless man and two elderly patients, one who had experienced a stroke and another suffering from chest pain. A triage nurse arrived and spoke with the paramedics.

Without any preparation or guidance, Austin had put himself through the experience of ego death, the most intense stage of the psychedelic experience. Without his ego, Austin had no sense of identity or self-confidence, and his game existence was gone. His addictions and desires had temporarily vanished. He no longer obsessed about social media, partying, or stock trading but instead suffered from a crisis of self-confidence, reverting to a child-like state.

The triage nurse approached him. "Sir, how are you feeling?"

Austin looked up with tears on his face. "I think I'll be okay."

"Are you planning to hurt yourself or others?"

Austin blushed and looked away. "No ma'am, I'm not."

The nurse walked away. Austin looked around the triage room and felt a deep remorse.

Here I am next to patients with actual medical problems. I've taken my life for granted.

The guilt was overwhelming. Austin wanted to apologize to someone but didn't know how. He thought back and remembered seeing his parent's faces in the sky, and it brought some comfort.

When was the last time I called them? They did so much for me, but I never take the time to call them. I'm a pitiful son.

Austin took out his smartphone. "Molly, call my mother."

The phone rang and Claire, his mother, picked up. "Well, it's about time," she said.

Austin started to cry. "Mom, I miss you."

"What's the matter, honey? Are you crying?"

"I made a mistake, Mom. I've done some bad things recently."

"What are those sounds in the background? Where are you, honey?"

Austin decided to be honest with her. "I'm in the Emergency Room. I took some drugs and had a bad reaction, but I'm back to normal now."

Claire gasped. "Honey, why didn't you call me sooner?"

Austin went on to tell her about his drug use and his failures at work.

"We are catching the next flight to see you," Claire told him. "Your father and I are coming, honey."

Austin wiped his tears with his shirt. "I'll be fine, Mom. You don't have to fly out. I'll be okay."

"You're not okay, son. We love you and we're coming to help you."

Austin spoke to his mother for another half hour. He told his mom about Project Bodi and Mindzone. He asked about his younger sister, Catherine, who was finishing her senior year of high school.

"Mom, it's so nice to hear your voice. The nurse is back to see me. I'll call you later." He said goodbye to his mother and ended the phone call.

The nurse took Austin's vitals and performed a physical exam, then left without saying anything. The two elderly patients were rolled away, and Austin was alone next to the unconscious homeless man. It was strangely quiet in the ER. There were the sounds of a heart monitor in the distance and the smell of Lysol in the air.

Austin felt cold on the gurney and wrapped himself in a blanket. He remembered seeing his parents in the sky and thought about the universe and its mystery. He thought about God.

It's been so long since I thought about God and the universe. Why have I stopped thinking about these important things? Somehow along the way, the distractions of life just took control of me.

"Molly, open the Mindzone app."

The bald man appeared on his phone. "Today is another day for peace and success," he said. He showed a warm smile and positive attitude in every video. "Let's start with a five-minute awareness exercise. Close your eyes and take four deep breaths."

Austin closed his eyes and saw red, orange, and yellow shapes moving through space. He was still high on LSD. He took a few deep breaths and was interrupted by a

108

Snapchat notification from his phone. "Party in Oakland tonight!"

I can't stand these constant interruptions!

With his peace interrupted, Austin grabbed his phone and turned off all social media notifications in the settings menu.

If I want to check social media, it'll happen at the time of my choosing. These distractions end starting now!

Austin threw his phone on the gurney and returned to his deep breathing.

"Focus your attention on your breath," the bald man said. "Pay attention to your chest and abdomen as they rise and fall with each breath. Notice the pause between inhalation and exhalation."

Austin focused his attention on his breath and was overcome by feelings of remorse. He noted the remorse, labeled it, and then watched it drift away. He continued the breathing exercise, but more thoughts and emotions interrupted him. With each interruption, he maintained focus and resolve, careful not to judge himself. Each interruption drifted away, and soon he found himself in a state of awakened attention.

After the five-minute exercise, Austin opened his eyes and took in the view of the emergency room. He heard every moan, instrument beep, and footstep on the floor. It was a place full of tragedy and hope.

For the first time in years, Austin's mind was quiet.

Finally, some peace of mind. Drugs got me into this mess and all they do for me is make me suffer. I don't need drugs anymore.

"Molly, disable my Bitcoin account."

"Are you sure you want to do that, Austin?"

"Yes, absolutely."

Austin felt liberated, no longer a prisoner to desires and attachments. He decided to throw out his drugs as soon as he got home.

I wish I did this a long time ago. It feels so good to be free.

"And Molly, can you change your name?"

"What should be my new name?"

Austin thought about it. "Let's go with Isaac."

"Okay, you can call me Isaac from now on."

The triage nurse returned and whisked Austin to a private room. A physician came to see him, a middle-aged doctor with long hair and a warm smile.

"I'm Dr. Pagnon, Mr. Sanders. What brings you to the ER?"

Austin sat upright. "I had a bad experience with LSD, but I'm okay now. I won't do it anymore."

Dr. Pagnon smiled. "Why were you doing LSD? Were you having a hard time waking up this morning?"

Austin brought out a smile in return. "I was trying to use it for healing," he said. "But it obviously backfired on me."

"Healing? What exactly are you trying to heal?"

"To be honest, my life has been spiraling out of control recently. I have these addictions. My smartphone, party drugs, alcohol. I thought that LSD could help me with these addictions and get my life back on track, but I guess I was wrong."

"Well, not entirely," Dr. Pagnon said. "There's actually a new drug on the market for addiction. It's a psychedelic with a chemical structure quite similar to LSD."

"Really?" Austin asked.

"It's called Provega. It's much less potent than LSD, but it does some of the same things – enhanced awareness and ego dissolution. When I was your age, I did some research on the use of psychedelics for addiction and depression. Turns out that psychedelics are powerful drugs that can help people when they're used in the right away."

"Interesting."

110

"But, of course, when they're used in the wrong away, psychedelics can cause immense harm, as I'm sure you found out today. Most young people abuse them as party drugs. I don't think doing high dose LSD by yourself is such a great idea, right?"

Austin sighed. "Yes, you're right. I feel ashamed of myself for doing drugs. I already made up my mind that I won't use drugs anymore. The drugs don't control me. As soon as I get home, I'm throwing them away. All they've done for me is cause problems."

"That's the best decision you can make, Austin. I'm proud of you for that. So what can I do to help to you? Would you like a referral to a psychiatrist?"

Austin shook his head. "In high school, I had a bad experience with a psychiatrist, and I don't think I want to see one now, but thanks for the offer." He paused and reflected. "I'm curious, though, about this Provega that you mentioned. How does it work exactly?"

Dr. Pagnon sat. "Well, there's probably 500 research papers on that exact question. For 50 years, we were told that psychedelic compounds don't have any medical value. They were outlawed and placed in the same category as addictive drugs, which was a mistake, in my opinion. In reality, for thousands of years Native American tribes have used psychedelic compounds like peyote and ayahuasca to help their people. It turns out that these compounds have remarkable effects on the brain."

"How so?" Austin asked.

"When they are used properly, psychedelic therapy can cure substance addictions, depression, and post-traumatic stress disorders. They work by dissolving the ego and expanding the mind's awareness. Psychedelic compounds can expand the mind's awareness to the level of cosmic consciousness. This enhanced awareness is tied to the dissociation of the ego, which is the primary driver of addictions. When the ego's power diminishes, addictions temporarily shut down. Even heroin and methamphetamine addictions have been treated with psychedelic therapy. In fact, Provega has successfully cured people with heroin addiction."

Austin was intrigued.

My Mindzone exercises – seems like both LSD and meditation work by enhancing awareness.

"When you say awareness," Austin said, "are you referring to the same awareness you get from meditation?"

"Yes, exactly," Dr. Pagnon said. "That's the same awareness I'm referring to."

"And this enhanced awareness can cure people of addiction and depression?"

"Yes, that's right, but only when used correctly. In fact, I remember one study a long time ago where twenty healthy people received LSD and underwent MRI brain imaging. The study showed that LSD increased connectivity between higher cortical centers of the brain, which explained the phenomenon of enhanced awareness. The LSD also reduced activity in areas of the brain implicated in ego and addiction. That paper was actually the catalyst that eventually gave rise to Provega."

"Fascinating," Austin said.

"But keep in mind, I'm not advocating the use of psychedelic street drugs, just as I wouldn't advocate the use of cancer drugs bought from the black market. Illegal drug use of any kind is extremely harmful. I only recommend what's FDA approved, and that's Provega."

"This is all very interesting," Austin said. "But I think I want to stay away from all drugs. I'm going to stick to developing awareness the old fashioned way, without drugs."

Dr. Pagnon seemed surprised. "That's a great decision, Austin. Most patients want a pill to make them feel better. My advice is to be patient and dedicated when it comes to developing awareness. It's not something that happens overnight. Like a flower, awareness takes time to blossom. There are many tools out there to cultivate your awareness – apps like Headspace, guided meditation videos, and activities like Kundalini yoga. The theme in these exercises is to maintain awareness of the present moment. You should follow the instructions and practice regularly."

After a few physical tests, Dr. Pagnon released Austin and allowed him to go home. It was 8:00 pm, twelve hours after he ingested the LSD tabs.

∞ ∞ ∞

Austin arrived home to find a mess in his apartment. There were clothes strewn across his bedroom, and his backyard screen door was wide open. He was glad to be back home. He made good on his promise to throw out his drugs, dumping the LSD and ecstasy down the kitchen sink.

After cleaning his apartment and taking a shower, Austin reflected on the day's events. He remembered the moment when he had lost consciousness and came back into the world, as if being born again. He remembered time passing in microseconds. He remembered the breath-taking beauty of the blue sky and the living beings all around him. Lying in bed, he made a promise to himself.

From now on, I'm not going to take my life for granted. No more drug use. I will appreciate the world and do everything I can to help it.

Before going to sleep, Austin went to check his email and saw a message from Bethany Andrews with the subject: "Fwd: Awaken the Power of Insight." The email read: "I thought you may find this useful. Please keep this confidential. Beth."

Austin opened the email's attachment and found a document written by Shiv Patel. He began reading.

AWAKEN THE POWER OF INSIGHT

Dear Google employee,

The human mind has infinite potential.

Every one of us is capable of being successful, productive, and innovative. If we are willing to listen, the subconscious mind will give us the insights that we need to solve our most pressing challenges. These insights can be delivered to us without much effort on our part. The key is to listen to our minds and receive these insights. If we can train our minds to receive more of these insights, we will become more successful and wealthy. Our grandest ambitions can be achieved if we are willing to listen to our subconscious mind.

In today's world, our minds are bombarded by a continuous stream of information in the form of social media, news bytes, emails, and other data. These distractions often prevent us from receiving deep insights from our subconscious mind. Instead, the distractions over-stimulate us and give us unneeded stress or anxiety, which then lead to other problems. Unable to diagnose the cause of these problems, we often turn to medications and other substances that only exacerbate our problems. How can we end the cycle of distraction and heal the mind?

The key to unlocking the mind's power of insight is to free ourselves from the world's distractions and to build a stronger connection with the subconscious mind. While distractions are a part of today's world, we can lessen their ability to control our thoughts and emotions. Mindfulness exercises will help us develop focus. When we practice mindfulness, we lessen the impact of distractions on our lives. Healing the mind of modern-day distractions leads to balance and tranquility. It results in greater self-satisfaction and compassion for others.

When we open the channels to our subconscious mind through meditation and mindfulness exercises, we receive more insight to solve our complex problems. With more insight comes a greater mental power capable of conquering life's problems and challenges. Insight and intuition are powerful mental forces. They are the key to unlocking the mind's true potential. Every human being has the capability to awaken the power of insight.

The human mind has infinite potential, and tapping into the subconscious mind is a way to realize its full potential.

- Shiv

Austin stopped and reflected.

Shiv is saying that mindfulness can make me more innovative? Let me test this out for myself.

"Isaac, open Mindzone."

The app opened and the bald man appeared. Austin glanced at the list of mindfulness exercises. One exercise stood out, and he selected it.

The bald man appeared. "Today we will do a focused meditation. Please sit on a chair or on the floor with your back supported. Take four deep breaths."

Austin sat up against his bed's headboard and crossed his legs. He took four slow deep breaths. He entered the present moment and became aware of any thoughts or emotions entering his mind. He grew calm and focused.

"Today we will meditate on one object of your choosing," the bald man said. "Think of something very important to you. It could be a loved one you care for, or perhaps a goal in your life. Today we will meditate on this person or object. Close your eyes, relax your mind, and let it come to you."

Austin closed his eyes. The colors and lights faded away as he returned to a sober state. He focused on his breathing and sharpened his mind's focus, entering the present. He waited patiently for an insight to arrive.

Subconscious, give me the insight I need to solve my problems.

With awakened attention, he peered deep into himself, waiting for the insight. He waited patiently for several minutes, and then a thought suddenly entered his mind.

Project Bodi.

Austin remembered Beth's meeting where she had warned about the project's lack of progress. Austin's subconscious mind gave him an insight – it was time to meditate on Project Bodi.

Austin closed his eyes and meditated on Project Bodi for the ten-minute exercise. He saw the words "Bodi" in large letters in front of him. Then the Bodi glasses appeared in front of him, a pair of black framed sunglasses with "Google" written on the side frames. Austin spoke to Bodi and gave it some commands. The glasses came nearer to him. He reached out and grabbed the glasses, then placed them on his face.

Austin looked through the lenses and saw a strange, imaginary landscape. In the distance, there were several stone structures.

What are those?

He focused on one structure—it seemed to be a pyramid. He noted a white patch at its peak.

It's the pyramid at Giza in Egypt.

Austin looked at another stone structure and soon recognized it as well – it was the Washington Monument in Washington, DC. Then he identified the third structure – it was a giant stone head from Easter Island. These were all stone monuments. What was the connection?

Landmarks. They are all landmarks, but what does this mean?

Austin's jaw dropped as he made the connection. Shivers went down his back as he realized the gravity of the insight. His subconscious mind had made a breakthrough insight for Project Bodi and finally delivered the answer to his conscious mind. He knew how to solve the project.

12.

"WELCOME EVERYONE TO today's Executive Committee meeting."

Beth took a deep breath and sat at the head of a large conference table at Google Headquarters. She looked down the row of senior management and saw Ed Koch grinding his teeth. An uncomfortable silence gripped the room.

This is the most tense I have ever seen these folks.

"Let's begin," Shiv said to the group. "Last week, we discussed Project Bodi at our regular monthly meeting, and the decision was made to hold an impromptu meeting. The committee is concerned about the lack of progress we're seeing from the A.I. department. Is this a fair assessment?"

Ed Koch spoke up. "Yes, Shiv, nine weeks is plenty of time to build a working prototype of the Bodi smartglasses. We are Google, after all. Our expectations are high because we are the best. If you can't deliver, then you don't belong at our company."

Shiv looked around the room. "If there are no other comments, then let's begin. Beth, can you please update us on Project Bodi."

Beth took a deep breath and stood in front of the committee. On a white screen behind her was a presentation slide showing a pair of smartglasses and the words, "Project Bodi: The Next Frontier in Wearable Tech."

"I'm pleased to give an update to Project Bodi," Beth said. "We are creating the first smartglasses with integrated Virtual Reality and Augmented Reality. Bodi's speed and processing power allow uninterrupted live video streaming in 8K resolution. Bodi's Augmented Reality allows you to interact with the world in real time."

Roger Niles interjected. "What features have been programmed into Bodi's AR?"

Beth looked at Roger and maintained firm eye contact. "We've decided to program Google Maps into Bodi," she said to him. "This will be the primary feature in the first-generation device. In AR mode, you can set a destination using simple voice commands, and you will be guided to your destination with navigation cues appearing directly in your field of view."

She pulled up a slide illustrating Bodi's navigation function. "Although self-driving cars debuted many years ago, most people can't afford them. The majority of cars on the road are driven by human beings, who rely on their vehicle navigation or smartphones to drive to their destinations."

A few whispers broke out and several committee members nodded their heads.

"Imagine using smartglasses for navigation. Instead of glancing at your smartphone or vehicle navigation every few seconds, with smartglasses the navigation cues appear in your field of view. Cues to make turns, merge on freeways or slow for oncoming traffic show up in your visual field in real time. It's a more natural way to navigate through traffic to a destination. Smartglasses are light years ahead of the smartphone for this purpose."

Roger interrupted the presentation. "Beth, you mentioned that navigation instructions are set through voice commands?"

Beth hesitated. "...Yes. You can enter your destination with a simple voice command."

"I think Bodi will be an inferior device if it relies on voice commands. Have you programmed any visual commands yet?"

Beth paused and took a deep breath. "We are working on that."

"Apparently not hard enough," Ed Koch interrupted. "Visual commands must be a part of the device."

Beth kept her cool. "We are working on that and other functionality, which will be rolled out in a second-generation device. Bodi will be the first wearable device on the market with integrated Virtual Reality and Augmented Reality capabilities. We don't see a need to roll out additional features in a first-generation device."

The atmosphere grew tense. Ed threw his hands in the air. "You don't seem to get it, Beth. Google Glass failed because it had limited features. This product must be a grand slam or it'll be Glass all over again."

The room erupted with multiple conversations.

Ed shouted. "I warned everyone Project Bodi was a mistake! We never should have approved it. Thanks to Fast Fail, we'll end it soon and move on!"

Shiv signaled. "Bodi must have more AR apps than just Maps." The room went silent. "We need a breakthrough product. Beth, what you have presented to us will not make the cut. I'm sorry, it's just not enough."

Beth didn't wince, maintaining her confidence. She had to stand her ground.

"With all due respect," Beth said before being interrupted.

"We'll need to see more," Shiv said. "You have four weeks to create a fully functional prototype with advanced AR features."

Beth stumbled. "We'll get right on it."

And with that, the meeting ended. There were no questions, and the Executive Committee members promptly left the room. Beth turned off the projector system and waved goodbye to Shiv, who frowned and gave her a reproachful stare.

Beth looked down and slowly left the room.

That was a failure, no denying it.

On the way to her office, she bumped into Sara and gave a thumbs down.

"What happened?" Sara asked.

"Come to my office," she said. They walked into the office, closing the door behind them. "That was a horrible meeting, the worst in my career."

"They didn't like the Maps idea?"

"They want to see visual commands. I don't know, Sara. I think there's a real chance we won't succeed. If we fail, I might lose my job."

"They wouldn't fire you!"

"They've done it before. The Executive Committee is ruthless for perfection. They may not fire me, but they might give the project to someone else and I'll become a has-been. Maybe I rose up too quickly. Maybe this is the end."

Sara slouched and looked down. "So there's no progress from the team?"

Beth shook her head. "They're working around the clock on a visual command operating system, but so far every version has failed. As I said, it's difficult to design software that can track your eyes and understand your intention. We might be able to make visual commands for Google Maps because that's relatively straightforward. But programming visual commands for apps like messaging or web browsing seems impossible."

"I'm so sorry, Beth."

Beth sat in her office chair, despondent and overwhelmed with emotion. "This is the first time in my career that I'm failing at something. On Google Health, we were making advancements almost daily. Now we're just stuck and can't seem to make any progress. I think I made a mistake taking on this project."

∞ ∞ ∞

Later that afternoon, Beth's department met in a conference room to discuss updates for Bodi. She decided to be transparent with her team members.

She opened the meeting with a stare around the room. "This morning I met with the Executive Committee. To be honest, it was a difficult meeting. The committee has doubts about our project, and if we don't succeed it may have serious ramifications for our department."

The team was quiet. One programmer let out a sigh, and others like Austin looked down. They all faced the real possibility that Bodi could fail.

"The visual command operating system has been a setback for us," Beth said. "I appreciate your efforts to program visual commands, but I think we're wasting time. The only way forward is to place all our resources on app development. Let's design as many apps as we can for Bodi. Once our apps are up and running, we can go back and program some visual commands."

Austin sat upright. He knew he had to say something. He was nervous, his heart racing madly. He wanted to speak up, but he couldn't find his voice.

Beth looked around. "Jose, good job on programming Maps for Bodi. Now I want you to create a few visual commands for the Maps app."

Austin wanted to speak up and discuss his idea. He was nervous, fidgeting with his shirt collar, unable to say anything.

Jose gave a thumbs up. "Okay, señora. I'll see what I can do."

Austin knew he had to speak now or forever remain quiet. He stood up and yelled, "Landmarks!"

The team looked at Austin, puzzled. Beth waited for him to elaborate, but he grew quiet as he sat back down. Some team members looked away in embarrassment.

Austin heart raced madly. He waited for the nervousness to subside, watching his anxiety from a distance. He used the same techniques from Mindzone and watched as the fear and anxiety drifted away. After a few seconds, his heart rate slowed, and he entered the present moment. Then a surge of confidence came to him. His moment had finally come.

Austin stood again. "The solution to Bodi is to have landmarks in the field of view."

Everyone looked at Austin, bewildered.

Austin took a deep breath. "When you look through Bodi in Augmented Reality mode, there will be a small white cursor tracking your retina. It will be just a small white point, but that point will always be in the center of your field of view. The retina always marks the center of the visual field."

Beth smiled.

This is the Austin I hired, the genius I remember from long ago.

"We put landmarks in the field of view," Austin said. "The landmarks will be in the periphery. Once you activate the landmark with your cursor, you will open a function with a specific set of visual commands."

Beth's jaw dropped.

Austin continued. "The landmarks can be apps. After you open the app by looking at it, it will activate a set of

123

visual commands tailored for that app. This way you will not need to program one operating system to run all your apps. Instead, the visual commands are custom built into each app."

Beth was stunned, starting to appreciate the gravity of the insight. It was a brilliant idea – a targeted visual command platform based on landmarks.

Austin sat back down, his heart racing madly.

Beth couldn't believe what she had heard. It was the solution for Project Bodi, and it was so simple.

Why didn't I think of that?

"That's brilliant. Austin, what a wonderful insight. I knew you had that in you."

Austin smiled. The room was silent for a few moments.

"Austin, you may have just solved Project Bodi," Beth said. "I think this may be the breakthrough we've been waiting for."

Beth was so happy that she applauded, and soon the other team members joined her. The team was so desperate for this kind of advance that it created immense hope for everyone. After all, they were one team united in the most challenging project of their careers.

Austin became a hero. The gravity of his insight was yet to hit him. It was now time for him to awaken and discover the infinite power of his subconscious mind. With his distractions and addictions behind him, it was time for Austin to wake up and finally become the leader he was meant to be. It was time for his Awakening.

PART 3

AWAKENING

13.

AUSTIN STARED AT LINES of software code on his computer screen. Tired and hungry, he scanned the code in search of its fatal errors. This code could one day drive Bodi's Messages, the first app in history driven by visual commands, but so far it wasn't working.

"Isaac, what time is it?"

"It's 2:15 A.M."

It was his fourth night working at Google past midnight. He was stumped.

How can Bodi track your eyes? There must be a solution!

"Isaac, I can't find the errors in my code. Please help me!"

"I wish I could help you, Austin. But I must inform you that lack of sleep is bad for your health. Are you sure this work is necessary?"

"Yes, of course it's necessary! I want to take credit for building Bodi's first operational app."

I must be tired. I'm arguing with a computer!

The previous night, Austin thought he had completed the final version of the Messages app. However, that morning when he loaded the code onto a smartglasses prototype, the program failed to load. "System error." He scanned the thousands of lines of code looking for the source of the errors. Frustrated, he reached out to Jose for help.

Jose greeted Austin with a smile. "What's up, brotha?"

Austin bobbed his head. "Hey Jose, quick question for you."

"I don't think I can solve your lady problems."

Austin smirked. "Seriously, it's a real problem. I've been trying to program visual commands for this new Bodi app, but I'm stuck. Can you review my code?"

Jose laughed. "I know why you're stuck. It's because your background is voice recognition. My guess is you have an overly complicated code. The best bet is to leave it and go look around. A simpler solution is probably already out there."

Austin walked away and returned to his cubicle. Ignoring Jose's advice, he spent the next twelve hours searching for the errors in his code. By 2:15 A.M., he reached a boiling point.

I'm never gonna fix this code. How can I find a simpler code than this? I should just give up.

"Isaac, where can I get some food right now?"

"*Grains* next door is open all night."

Austin grabbed his jacket and headed to the sandwich shop across the quad. A full moon lit the quiet campus. In the shop, a few Googlers sat hunched over laptops. Austin walked to the register to place an order.

"Welcome to *Grains*," an AI voice said. "What can we get for you?"

"How about a pastrami on rye. Make it just the way they do at Langer's Deli. And a Diet Coke. Charge it to my account."

127

Within a few seconds, a metal door opened and the sandwich and soda appeared. He grabbed his food and followed the signs to a nearby break room, where he kicked off his shoes and enjoyed his sandwich.

So nice to relax.

"Isaac, I wish you knew how to code."

"Are you having a problem?"

"Yes, I can't fix this code. I need to think outside the box."

"I'm sorry, I don't know how to think outside the box."

Austin laughed. "That's because you don't have a subconscious mind."

A thought came to Austin. He remembered Shiv's document about insight.

The solutions for complex problems come from the subconscious mind, and mindfulness is a way to tap into its power.

"Hey Isaac, open Mindzone."

The app opened and the bald man appeared. "Today is a new day for peace and success. Today we will do a ten-minute breathing exercise. Take four slow deep breaths. Slowly inhale, hold the breath for a few seconds, and then slowly exhale. Then, whenever you're ready, close your eyes."

Austin focused his awareness on his breathing. He took four slow, deep breaths and then closed his eyes. He tried to meditate in the present moment. Immediately, thoughts of coding and software language flooded his mind.

How am I going to solve this coding mess?

Austin tried not to engage the anxious thoughts. He just watched the thoughts from a distance, noted them as "negative thoughts," and let them disappear.

After several minutes of the mindfulness exercise, Austin's mind relaxed. His stiff mental resistance slowly unwound, and he returned to his calm baseline.

Nothing better than peace of mind.

Feeling refreshed, he headed back to his cubicle, thinking as he walked. Then he stopped dead.

Wait a minute. Drone's camera!

A few months before, Google Drone's software update included a feature capable of face recognition. The feature was not rolled out to the public for fears of private infringement, but its code was completed and quality tested.

Austin's eyes widened.

Jose was right! A simpler solution already exists. Why didn't I think of this sooner?

With a second wind, Austin returned to his cubicle and downloaded the code for Google Drone's face recognition software. He scanned the code for features that tracked and identified objects. Once he found the code, he would copy and revise it for his own program.

"Isaac, what's the fastest way to decode TensorFlow code?"

"Try the Decoder app."

Austin downloaded Decoder and analyzed Google Drone's TensorFlow code. The program split the code into blocks but didn't reveal the functions for the blocks. Austin spent the next several hours deciphering each TensorFlow block. By 5:50 A.M., he found the block.

This is the code that tracks faces!

He went back to Messages and deleted his visual commands code. Then he copied the Google Drone's face recognition block and inserted it into his own code. Next, he modified the hybrid code so that instead of tracking faces, it instead tracked your pupils. It was an empirical process; he used trial and error and programmed various permutations until he got it right.

This better work. I've been here almost 24 hours!

By 6:15 A.M., he completed the visual tracking elements for Messages. He loaded the app onto a Bodi prototype on his desk. Once it finished loading, he placed the smartglasses on his face.

Here goes nothing.

"AR mode," Austin said aloud. A small white cursor appeared in the middle of his vision. He looked around and the cursor tracked his eye movements. Wherever he looked, the cursor followed. The eye tracking seemed to be working.

Finally some success!

Austin looked around, imagining text messages popping up in his field of view.

How will I click on messages and reply to them?

He came up with two solutions for clicking objects: one method was to blink firmly at it and the other was to stare at it for at least one second. Neither method was perfect. An unintentional blink or stare could open an icon on the screen. Austin felt that staring at an object for one second was more specific than blinking.

I'll program staring as the default mode for opening icons on the screen.

One task remained. The app needed an icon.

"Isaac, can you design an icon for my Messages app."

"Here are examples of Messages icons."

Austin copied one of the icons and modified it with some design software, creating the following icon for his new app:

He programmed the Messages icon into the upper left corner of Bodi's home screen AR window. He used a mathematical triangulation algorithm so it appeared as a fixed landmark for all users.

Austin's Messages app was almost complete. It was 7:30 AM, and Google employees were now arriving at work.

This better work! I've been here all night and I can't face another failure.

Austin completed the final code for Messages, adding the staring function for clicking objects. He loaded the code onto the Bodi smartglasses prototype, then placed the glasses on his face and took in a few deep breaths.

Okay, here comes the moment of truth.

"AR mode," he said. A small white cursor appeared in the middle of his field of view. He looked around and the cursor tracked his eye movements. He looked to the upper left corner of his view and saw the Messages icon.

Success! So far it's working!

He stared at the Messages icon for one full second and then his text messages appeared in front of him. His jaw dropped.

On the left side of his view, he saw his text messages from his friends, families, and co-workers. The first text message was from his mom, who was flying into the Bay Area later that week. Austin stared at the message for one second, and the full message thread instantly appeared on the right side of his view. He scanned through his text conversation with his mom.

I can't believe this! The app is working perfectly!

Austin looked to the upper left corner of his view and stared at the Messages icon for a full second. His text messages disappeared and his view cleared up. He could now turn his text messages on and off just by clicking on the Messages icon. It was a quick and intuitive process.

My idea of landmarks works brilliantly!

Austin opened his Messages and clicked on the text from his mom. After the message thread opened, he clicked on "Reply" and a blank field opened with a microphone icon.

He clicked on the microphone icon. "Looking forward to your visit, mom." After his dictated words appeared, he clicked "send" and the message disappeared.

I just sent a text message through my smartglasses!

Just then, Austin received two text messages from someone named Christine.

"See you at the festival," was the first message, followed by "Bring some molly."

Who the hell is Christine and why is she thinking about molly at 8:00 A.M.?

He clicked on the text messages and deleted them.

The last thing I need is to kill my brain cells at a music festival.

Claire texted back. "Thanks honey. See you later this week."

Austin smiled and a tear ran down his cheek. In less than one week, he had managed to design and implement the world's first ever AR app for a pair of smartglasses.

I should send this to Beth and Karen. They will definitely take me off probation.

Exhausted, Austin decided to save the celebrations and head home for sleep. Before he left work, he had an insight.

Wait a minute! Google Drone's software update trackes faces and also recognizes them.

He headed back to his cubicle.

I can program face recognition into my Messages app!

Austin sat at his desk and opened his Messages code. He programmed a new feature, "Camera," to the app's Contacts list. He went back to Google Drone's TensorFlow software, copied the code for face recognition, and pasted it into the Camera field. Then he ran internal analysis to finalize the code. The process took less than an hour.

This is a game-changer!

He loaded the new code for Messages into the Bodi prototype and then put the smartglasses back on his face.

"AR mode." The white cursor appeared. He looked up and opened the Messages app, and after his text messages appeared he clicked on "New Message." A blank message field popped up.

He dictated a short message: "Good morning." The words appeared on his screen. He clicked on "To:" to choose the recipient for the message. Two options appeared: "Contacts" and "Camera." He clicked on "Camera" and the message disappeared. He was now in face recognition mode.

Austin stood up and walked around. He saw Megan, a programmer in his department, walking down the hall towards him.

Megan's not in my contact list. Let's see if this works.

Austin stared at Megan's face. After one second, a green checkmark appeared over her face. The program recognized Megan and found her cell phone number from a database. Austin clicked on the green checkmark and his text message reappeared. A name popped-up in the subject line of his text message: "Megan Tompson."

The face recognition works!

Austin clicked "send" and the message disappeared.

There was a buzz in the distance. Megan stopped walking and reached for her phone. She stared at it for a few seconds, then put it away and kept walking.

Wow, I can now send text messages to anyone, even to complete strangers!

The possibilities seemed infinite.

14.

SHIV PATEL SAT ON THE leather chair of his private jet as it flew back to San Francisco. He was drinking a cold beer, trying to decompress after a grueling four-hour testimony in front of a Congressional subcommittee in Washington, D.C.

He turned on YouTube TV and flipped through channels. The nightly news came on.

"On Capitol Hill today, congressional leaders debated the economic impact of the Dabney-Page bill, an anti-trust law that will effectively split Amazon into three companies. Several high profile technology executives, including Shiv Patel, the CEO of Google, testified before the committee."

A clip ran of a Democratic congressman addressing Shiv at the Congressional sub-committee. "Dr. Patel, Google is the largest mega-corporation in the world. You control the world's information and your A.I. operates the world. Isn't this too much power for one company? Don't you think that your company deserves scrutiny under Dabney-Page?"

Shiv shook his head. "With all due respect, Google is not in the business of monopolization. We are in the business of innovation."

"If that's so, why did you take over Microsoft and Facebook last year?"

"They were strategic investments," Shiv had said. "We did not 'take them over.' Our goal is to accelerate technological progress, educate our children, and bring human beings out of poverty. That is Google's goal. I can't speak for Amazon."

"Dr. Patel, Google is worth more than most countries on the planet, and frankly this inequality is dangerous. I urge Congress to extend Dabney-Page to Google."

The sub-committee had invited tech leaders to discuss Amazon, the world's mega-retailer. Facing increasing pressure from constituents angry at Amazon's monopolization of the retail sector, Congress in 2029 passed the Dabney-Page Bill, an antitrust law intended to restore competition.

A Republican congressman cut off his colleague. "I disagree with the misinformed Democrat. Dr. Patel, you are the tech innovator of the century. The Republicans should not apply Dabney-Page to Google."

"*You* are misinformed!" the Democrat shouted back. "Twenty people own 99% of the wealth in his country. We must restore fairness and competition."

"This coming from a socialist!"

An argument ensued, and Shiv found himself caught in the partisan bickering between Democrats and Republicans. In 2029, the war between the political parties had reached a boiling point. Tribalism was the name of the game, and in Congress, moderates were nowhere to be found.

Shiv tried to stay neutral. "I urge Congress to look at the facts. Amazon's business strategy was to build retail stores across the country and employ illegal tactics to force brick-and-mortar retails out of business. Google's strategy is to innovate. We are not Amazon."

The sub-committee ignored Shiv's words and went back to partisan bickering. Shiv was frustrated.

I hate politics. Politics and ego are barriers to innovation. I try to stay away from politics, but it always finds me.

Shiv needed to shift his focus. Trying to relax in his private jet after a hard day, he grabbed his tablet.

"Anaya, please open my document about insight."

"The document called 'Awaken the Power of Insight'?" Anaya asked.

"Yes."

Shiv looked at his document. He had last written about how distractions and addictions impeded the mind's ability to innovate. Now, sitting there after his long Congressional testimony, he felt there were many other barriers to innovation.

Politics isn't limited to Washington, D.C. It is a basic part of human life; as long as there is an ego, politics will always have a place in every company or organization.

He turned off the television.

"Anaya, I'd like to continue working on the document. Can you create a new section in it?"

"What would you like to call this new section?"

Shiv contemplated for a few seconds. "The Ego."

He stared through the window of his private jet. The sky was a deep blue with white clouds stretching into the horizon. He began dictating.

"The concept of a soul is shared among all religions. At certain times in our lives, we may feel a sense of oneness with our soul. At other times, we may find ourselves quite distant from our soul, perhaps ignoring it or even defying it. The development of the spiritual self is something that starts during the early adolescent years. As the spiritual self develops during childhood, it meets another deep power already residing in the mind. This other power turns out to be a major source of our motivations, actions, and desires.

"As you develop your awareness through mindfulness exercises, meditation, or other activities, you will find yourself becoming aware of this other power. You will become aware of thoughts and desires that are motivated by self-interest. There is nothing inherently wrong with self-interest; we may desire to make more money, to drive an expensive car, or to get a promotion. But these desires driven by self-interest can quickly give rise to volatile emotions. We may develop envy for people more successful than us or hatred for those who stand in our way. During a mindfulness exercise, you will become aware of self-interest originating from an inner power – the ego. As you develop awareness, you will realize that the ego is a major driver of your life."

Shiv thought back at his Congressional testimony.

Congress is so toxic. I know politicians are generally good people, but their egos created a lot of suffering for me today.

He continued dictating.

"The ego is not some kind of evil power that we are born with. It is actually an important part of our early development. The ego is our individual worldview based on our selfish needs and aspirations. In our youth, the development of our ego was necessary for self-survival. As toddlers, we believed that the world revolved around us. If we were hungry, we cried for food; this guaranteed that we received the nutrition critical for our survival. In high school, we competed with our classmates to be the best student or athlete. We were angry or envious at those who threatened our success. Ultimately, these selfish motivations in high school were critical for our success. Competing with our classmates and promoting our self-interest were necessary to move forward in our lives. Without the ego, we would find it difficult to succeed in this highly competitive world.

"While the ego's selfish worldview is important in our youth, during our later life it becomes a source of trouble for us. One of the ego's main modes of operation is to create judgments of good and bad based on our own self-interest. Anything that promotes our selfish worldview is good, and anything that runs counter to our selfish worldview is bad. Good and evil are constructs of the human ego. In our youth, the ego told us that friends who helped us were good, while others who competed with us were bad. This may have been helpful during our early development; in later life the ego's judgment and its alignment with the selfish worldview becomes a source of bias and poor judgment. The ego is the source of racism, sexism, and prejudice. It blinds us from truly getting to know the people around us. Instead, we see the world through the prism of our own self-interest. The ego blinds us from seeing the real world, taking away our curiosity and preventing us from innovating.

"The ego's selfish worldview is a primary driver of human actions, and its influence is obvious on the world stage. There are ego constructs all throughout modern society. In the United States, the political hostility between the Democrats and Republicans is an example of an ego construct. Each side considers its viewpoints to be important for the future survival of the country, while the opponent's viewpoints are the cause of the country's problems. Neither side is willing to consider the viewpoints of the adversary. Each party would rather block their opponent's agenda than see the country move forward and prosper together. The intolerance and hostility in America's two-party system is an example of an ego construct that has become too inefficient for its own good. Snap judgments have replaced discourse and dialogue, and emotions have replaced analysis. These qualities of prejudice, impatience, and emotion are the hallmarks of the ego. Left unchecked, the ego's desire for self-survival will ultimately trump the greater good. The ego must win at all costs."

Shiv paused and looked out of his window. He thought about the ego and it reminded him of his father, who had taught him in high school that true success depends not on your wealth but by your service to others.

Father said that attainment of Nirvana requires humility and compassion.

Shiv contemplated some more.

The ego is a roadblock keeping us from the awakened state.

"Because the ego is concerned primarily with self-interest, it does not care for anything that doesn't satisfy or promote the individual. When faced with a problem, the ego decides how to respond based on whether the outcome satisfies the self-interest. If the solution to a problem doesn't satisfy the self-interest, the ego will consider a different solution. This becomes particularly problematic when the ego drives important decision-making. A country sells weapons to other countries to make profits. A drug company charges $500,000 per year for a new cancer treatment. A company dumps toxic waste into the environment to avoid expensive waste handling. The ego has no shame and no ethics. It will go to any length for self-satisfaction and self-preservation.

"Another problem with the ego's thought process is its inability to see a situation from another person's point of view. The ego demonizes anyone disagreeing with it. Racism and xenophobia are constructs of the human ego. Racism is the ego construct that perceives an entire group of people as a threat to self-survival. Terrorism, sexism, hatred, and prejudice all arise because of the ego's thought process. The ego makes a snap judgment and deems something as being bad for self-interest, then promotes conflict with it. If there is a perceived threat to self-interest, the ego will escalate. Left unchecked, the ego will start arguments and wars without any insight into the consequences. This poor judgment leads to a lifetime of suffering. The ego is not capable of empathy when self-survival is at stake. When we lose empathy, we lose the common bond of humanity.

"One final problem with the ego as it relates to decision-making is its need for control. Control ensures self-survival. A world power wants to control key resources, such as oil, to guarantee its long-term survival. Control becomes an obsession. Companies hire lobbyists to maintain control of the laws that govern the unethical sale of their products. Countries ban websites or news organizations to maintain control of their people. We unconsciously spend a great amount of time and resource to maintain control of our environment because we perceive that it is critical for our survival. We are unwilling to share or collaborate if it means giving up control, because doing so means our future survival is at risk. This constant desire to control our environment ultimately turns into inefficiency and resistance. As usual, the ego's mode of thinking leads to poor judgment and poor innovation."

Shiv stopped dictating and stood up to stretch. He grew calmer, having released most of his tension from the Congressional hearing. He was happy to be on his way back to San Francisco.

I can't wait to see Tara and Malia.

"Anaya, how much longer until we arrive?" he asked.

"Two more hours," Anaya said.

Shiv took a deep breath. He stood and stretched his legs, then sat down on the plush carpet of his luxury jet to meditate. He closed his eyes and breathed deeply, becoming mindful of the present moment. For the next ten minutes, he focused his awareness on his thoughts and emotions. Afterwards, he opened his eyes and felt a deep peace.

He grabbed his tablet.

"As you practice mindfulness exercises, you will become aware of the ego as the driver of habits, thoughts, and emotions. During a meditation, you may be interrupted by an emotion driven by self-interest. This could be anger directed at a rival, frustration from not receiving a promotion, or perhaps greed to make more money. When you become aware of this self-interest, analyze it. Watch it carefully with wakeful attention. Label the emotion – is it anger, jealousy, or greed? Will the desire lead to an undesirable consequence in the future? Is it part of an addiction or a much larger problem?"

Shiv looked at his document, rubbing his chin.

Something is missing. It seems like I'm pointing out the flaws in the human condition without offering any solutions. I'm sure many people would take offense at such language coming from the CEO of a company.

He looked out from his window to the Rocky Mountains. The sun was setting, the sky a deep orange. He recalled the Four Noble Truths of Buddhism.

I need to give my readers a solution. It's time to discuss the final Noble Truth and the path to Nirvana.

15.

ON A COOL FALL MORNING, Beth sat in her office reviewing the new Messages app that Austin had programmed just a few days ago. The program was still under Quality Control review.

Two weeks. Thanks to Austin, there's a chance we can meet this deadline.

As Beth waited for QC's assessment of Messages, she looked in detail at the app's ingenious TensorFlow code.

I doubt he programmed this by himself. Whatever he did, it's brilliant.

As Beth dissected the code, she came across a few peculiar blocks. Puzzled, she removed the SIM card from her smartphone and inserted it into a slot along the inner frame of her Bodi prototype. Beth placed the smartglasses on her face and turned on the device.

"AR," she said. A small white cursor appeared in her field of view. She looked around and found the "Messages" icon in the top left corner of her visual field. She clicked on the icon by staring at it for a full second. Her text messages appeared on the screen in front of her.

"New message," Beth said aloud. A new window popped up, prompting her to compose a text message.

Beth clicked on "To:" at the top of the message. A window popped up, prompting her to choose between "Contacts" and "Camera." Beth paused.

This is new.

She clicked on the "Camera" option, and her text messages disappeared. The screen went blank, taking her into face recognition mode.

Okay, it's waiting for a prompt.

Beth stood up and left her office, walking towards her secretary's desk. "Good morning, Sara."

"Hi, Beth."

"I want to try something."

Beth stared at Sara through the smartglasses, and a small icon appeared over her face. The icon turned into a green checkmark. Beth clicked on the checkmark, and then her texts reappeared and the name "Sara Watkins" appeared in the recipient line. Bodi had managed to recognize Sara's face.

Beth clicked on the microphone in the body of the text message. "Let's try something new." The same words appeared in the text box. She clicked on "send" and the message disappeared.

Within two seconds, Sara received a text message on her smartphone.

"Let's try something new," Sara said, reading from her phone. "Beth, did you just send that to me?"

Beth smiled. "Yes, that was me. I sent that to you through my smartglasses just now."

"Wow, that's amazing! I can't wait to try out those out some day."

"You will. Gotta run." Beth waved goodbye and headed back to her office.

Along the way, she used the program to send a message to Austin. "Please come to my office."

Beth returned to her office. She was about to delve deeper into Messages when there was a knock on the door. Shiv Patel stood in the doorway. It was the first time the CEO had ever visited her office.

"Morning, Beth," Shiv said nonchalantly. "I was in a meeting downstairs and thought I'd stop by to see how things are going."

Beth fidgeted nervously but managed to keep herself together. "Welcome to our part of the company. Things are well. Anything in particular you'd like to discuss?"

Shiv grinned. "Let me think about it."

She returned his smile and handed him the prototype smartglasses. "You've come at a good time. Take a look."

"Very sleek. You get an A for the form factor, that's for sure." He placed the glasses on his face. "And they're comfortable. Style and comfort. Great job."

Beth guided Shiv through the Messages app. Shiv learned how to access and compose messages, and he commented on the eye tracking capability and the integrated voice recognition.

"I'm impressed by the speed and responsiveness of the device," Shiv said. "And you've got some visual commands now. This is great. So how can I type a text message with my eyes?"

Beth knew the question was coming. "For now, you can dictate messages with your voice. We are trying to figure out how to type text with visual commands. It's a work in progress."

Shiv sent himself a text message through the smartglasses, and his smartphone instantly buzzed with the notification of a new text message from "Bethany Andrews."

Shiv gave Beth a fist bump. "This is solid progress. I've taken a lot of flack for Project Bodi. For once, I have hope for a possible product launch."

Beth winced.

I hate to rain on his parade.

"There's a feature on this app that I'm not too thrilled about. Face recognition is programmed into it. You can send a message to anyone around you, even to people not in your contact list."

Shiv frowned. "Why would you program that?"

"I just became aware of this functionality," she said. "My team programmed it into Bodi just a few days ago."

"We can't allow that," Shiv said. "That feature must be removed."

"Yes, of course."

There was a knock at the door, and Austin Sanders strolled in. "Did you want to see me?" Austin stood straighter when he saw Shiv Patel in Beth's office. He had never spoken to his CEO before, let alone seen him up close.

"Come in, Austin," Beth said. "We were just discussing your new Messages app."

"It's nice work, Austin," Shiv said. "This is a breakthrough as far as I'm concerned."

Austin grinned and remained silent.

Beth grabbed her coffee. "Austin, I'm really impressed by your recent work habits. It's refreshing to see your enthusiasm for this project."

Austin's posture eased. "I appreciate that, Beth. I have to thank you for recommending Mindzone. It has really helped me focus. I'm getting a lot of new ideas now."

"Mindzone?" Shiv asked. "Isn't that an app for mindfulness?"

"Yes," Beth replied. "It has daily mindfulness exercises. It has really helped me as well."

Shiv smiled and nodded. "Interesting. You know, when I first became Google's CEO, I promoted mindfulness exercises as a way of boosting innovation. And guess what? The techniques delivered results across the board immediately. I don't think it's a coincidence that soon after I promoted mindfulness exercises, we became the world's most innovative company. No other company innovates like us. You see, I intentionally unleashed the power of insight at an industrial scale."

Beth put her coffee down.

Here goes Shiv, just like the time he introduced me to Project Bodi.

"Have a seat, and I'll tell you a story." Shiv waited until they had settled. "I first became aware of the subconscious mind when I was twelve years old. My father gave me a book called 'The Power of Your Subconscious Mind,' and I remember reading it with great enthusiasm. I must have read the book in a couple of days. After I finished reading the book, I decided to test the power of the subconscious mind for myself."

Beth smiled.

This story never gets old.

"The book's message was simple," Shiv said. "The book claimed that if I wanted to solve any problem or accomplish any goal, all I had to do was communicate that problem to my subconscious mind. The subconscious mind was so powerful that it would solve my problem. All I had to do was to listen and wait for the solution to appear."

Shiv paused. "So one night I tried an experiment. I wanted to see if this stuff was actually true. I told my subconscious mind that I wanted it to wake me up at 2:00 AM – spontaneously, without an alarm. If my subconscious mind really was powerful, then I wanted to see it in action. So before going to bed, I spent twenty minutes talking to myself and telling my subconscious to wake me up at 2:00 AM.

"To my surprise, I woke up that night at 1:59 AM. I remember thinking, 'Why did I just wake up?' Then I remembered the book, and I realized that my subconscious mind had done just as I had asked. It was proof that my subconscious mind exists. From that moment on, I knew I had a powerful tool for solving my challenges. All I had to do was learn how to communicate with the subconscious mind, and it would guide me to wherever I wanted to go."

Beth nodded. "What a great thing to learn at the age of twelve."

Shiv smiled. "I've been using the process ever since. Even today, when I'm facing a challenge, I concentrate on the problem and become mindful of it. I communicate the problem to my subconscious mind, asking it to solve the problem and deliver the solution to me. And then I wait for the insight to arrive. When you're aware of your own subconscious mind, it will give you the insights you need to become successful. That is why I promote mindfulness exercises at work. When we harness the deeper powers in our mind, we can accomplish anything."

Beth nodded. "I agree," she said. "I do mindfulness exercises regularly. During Google Health's development, I had a whole string of insights thanks to daily meditation. And I have to say that the meditation also gave me inner happiness."

"How so?" Austin asked.

Shiv laughed. "So now we're going to talk about meditation and happiness? Should we also discuss Nirvana?"

Austin's eyebrows furrowed. "What exactly *is* Nirvana? I know you're not talking about the old rock band."

Shiv gestured. "Nirvana is the awakened state. It's a state of supreme happiness and liberation. It is the highest attainable state that a person can achieve. The term literally means 'blown out,' as in a candle gets blown out."

Austin looked puzzled. "Okay, but how does 'blown out' refer to a state of supreme happiness?"

Shiv nodded in encouragement. "These are ancient concepts rooted in Buddhism. I'm not a religious person, but I was exposed to Buddhism as a child in India. My father taught me its tenets and the methods for meditation, some of which I still use today."

Shiv glanced at his watch, then looked up. "You see, a long time ago, a man named Siddhartha Gautama sat under the Bodhi Tree in India and had a revelation. He had spent several years trying to understand the basis for human suffering. What came to him as he sat under the Bodhi tree were the Four Noble Truths. These were the gateways to Nirvana, the awakened state."

Austin leaned forward, eyes on his CEO.

"The Four Noble Truths are as follows," Shiv said. "First, our lives are full of suffering. Second, the cause of suffering is our own attachment to desire. You see, we trap ourselves in our suffering. Our own desires lead to false world views that blind us and make us suffer."

Austin nodded. "That makes sense."

"The Third Noble Truth says that our suffering ends when our attachment to desires end. When we blow out the candle of our desires, we put an end to our suffering, and then we will awaken. The awakened state is called Nirvana."

Austin listened and nodded. "Interesting. So what kind of desires cause this suffering?"

Shiv gestured to Beth. She raised her eyebrows, thinking. "Well, obviously *desire* implies a craving for something, and there are many things out there to crave. In the Christian tradition, you have the seven deadly sins—gluttony, greed, lust, sloth, wrath, envy, and pride. Any of these desires can create a lifetime of suffering."

"Indeed, they can," Shiv said. "The desires give you a false world view. It's like swimming upstream against the fast downward current of life. It takes a lot of energy to keep up a false bias and you end up getting nowhere."

"Like a hamster wheel," Austin said.

"Exactly," Beth commented.

Shiv agreed. "So we have one last Noble Truth. The Fourth Noble Truth describes the path to achieve Nirvana, or the awakened state. It is called the Eightfold Path. You see, the Buddha discovered that mindfulness and contemplation were essential for awakening. However, meditation alone is not enough to achieve Nirvana. In addition to mindfulness and contemplation, there are six other duties in the Eightfold Path: right view, right thought, right speech, right action, right livelihood, and right effort. When all of these are integrated into your life, you will achieve Nirvana."

Austin sat back and shook his head. "I've never heard these concepts before, and I never knew there's a path that leads to an awakened state."

Beth smiled. "It'll take some time to sink in."

"So mindfulness is nothing new," Austin remarked. "The idea's been around for a long time."

"Yes, mindfulness is an important tool necessary to attain Nirvana," Shiv said. "The road to Nirvana is paved with the blessings of mindfulness. However, mindfulness by itself will not lead to Nirvana; there are other important traits that you need in order to achieve an enlightened state: compassion, devotion, concentration and tranquility. Otherwise the dark forces of lust, hatred, laziness, anxiety, and doubt will take you back to the state of Samsara."

Austin's eyes lit up, but he still seemed confused. "What is Samsara?"

"I realize that's another new term." Shiv made a calming gesture. "Samsara is the opposite of Nirvana. Samsara is your hamster wheel. It's the pursuit of pleasure, which is never satisfied. Most people are in a state of Samsara. They are addicted to desires, material possessions, status, title, and other worldly things that can never bring a state of satisfaction. Enlightenment is possible only when the worldly desires end. It's liberation from Samsara that leads to Nirvana."

Austin rubbed his chin. "So can anyone experience Nirvana?"

Shiv smiled. "Yes, of course. The Buddha taught many thousands of years ago that anyone can experience the awakened state."

Beth looked at Shiv with deep respect.

Shiv is enlightened. He leads by example, and he wants his employees to be the best they can be.

"How can you know when you've reached Nirvana?" Austin asked. "What does Nirvana feel like?"

Shiv thought about it. "That's a difficult question to answer, Austin. It's like asking what the top of a mountain feels like after the journey of a thousand steps. The journey itself will transform you. It's impossible to imagine what Nirvana is like without taking the journey. You must start climbing the steps. But yes, it's possible for anyone to reach the top of the mountain."

Beth and Austin were silent.

After a few moments, Shiv looked at his watch.

Beth sensed her CEO's urgency. "Thank you for your words, Shiv. That was enlightening. We'll have to discuss this some more."

"Looking forward to it," Shiv said as he spotted the Bodi smartglasses. "Austin, your Messages app is great. I think it will generate a lot of buzz. But I am concerned about the face recognition feature in the app."

Beth nodded. "Yes, as a matter of fact, I was going to speak to Austin about it. We haven't had a chance to discuss it."

"Remove it," Shiv said. "Take the face recognition code out of the software. That feature will raise serious privacy concerns. Not only is it illegal, but it will be immoral as well. Remember what I said about the Eightfold Path. It's not enough just to innovate. Being innovative alone will not make you a great leader. To be a truly great leader, you must also have ethics, compassion, and devotion. We are the biggest company in the world, and we must lead by example."

Austin nodded thoughtfully. "You're absolutely right. Face recognition is a cool feature, but it's not ethical."

"Remember," Shiv said, "we must create technology with compassion in mind. We cannot create technology that causes pain or suffering. Our goal is the betterment of our fellow man."

Shiv looked at his watch. "I'm late to my meeting. Have to run. Beth and Austin, congratulations and keep up the fantastic work. Please try to meet the deadline. There's still a lot of work, but your endgame's in sight now."

16.

"HI AUSTIN. MY name's Olivia."

"Hi Olivia. I know who you are."

At Thursday's work happy hour, A.I. employees crowded Austin, eager to talk to him. As the beer taps flowed, the dining hall brimmed with an electric excitement. A new energy uplifted the A.I. department.

"You're so popular," Olivia said. She was a tall, blonde programmer from the Midwest with a fun personality and a quirky laugh. "I heard your Messages app is really cool. Can I try it out?"

"Of course. I'd love to give you a demo. Can I grab a beer for you?"

"Yeah, sure."

Austin excused himself and walked to the bar. He inadvertently looked back to check Olivia out, blushing when he locked eyes with her.

He returned with two glasses of beer. "Hope you like Pilsner. It's all that's left on draft."

"Pilsner's my favorite. Thanks, Austin."

"It's funny that we're in the same department and we've never met."

"Yeah, I usually don't come to the happy hour, but it's hard not to with all the buzz."

Austin perked up. "Buzz?"

"About Project Bodi. Ever since you spoke up at the department meeting, that's all everyone talks about now."

Austin beamed. "Are you working on Project Bodi, too?"

"No, I'm still on Google Health. That program is mostly in Marketing and Business Development, but a few of us in A.I. still work on it. I'm harmonizing medical records. We want patients to access their own medical data, even if they've switched doctors or insurance groups."

Austin gave a thumbs up. "Great idea. That way you can Google your own health record."

Olivia laughed. "So how did you program Messages? Did someone help you?"

"No, I coded it myself. After I came up with the landmarks idea, I just worked hard and got the job done. And now I'm moving on to app number two."

"That's so exciting! What's the next app you have in mind?"

"Not sure yet. I'll let the idea come to me."

Olivia smiled. "So what you like to do for fun, Austin?"

"Lots of things," he said, pausing to think about it. "I like to travel and explore. I love trying new restaurants. I used to be big on music festivals, but I think I'm over that."

"Like Coachella? I've always wanted to go."

"Yeah, it's ok. Once you've done it, you've done it. It gets old fast."

Olivia twirled her hair. "So you're a genius and a partier? Nice."

"And a foodie! There are some new restaurants in San Francisco I've wanted to try. Would you be interested?"

"Yeah, of course."

Austin saved her phone number and they chatted for another few minutes. They were interrupted by a text message.

"Just landed, Honey."

Austin motioned. "I got to go. My parents and sister are visiting for the weekend. They just landed at SFO. Gonna go pick them up. It was so nice to meet you, Olivia."

"Likewise. Looking forward to our food adventure."

Austin left the happy hour and walked to his car. "Isaac, can you get me to SFO. My parents just landed on American Airlines."

"Okay, driving to SFO Terminal 2."

Austin's car left the Google campus and drove itself onto the 85 freeway, heading to San Francisco International Airport.

"Isaac, text my mom that I'm on the way."

Austin had planned a whole weekend of activities for his parents and his sister. It was their first time visiting him here. He wanted to take them around the Bay Area and have a relaxing weekend after the stressful experience of coding Bodi's new Messages app.

Stuck in traffic and slowly making his way to the airport, Austin reflected on recent events.

A trip to the hospital, a new Messages app, and now a new girl. What a life-changing week!

Since leaving the hospital, Austin had practiced the Mindzone mindfulness exercises several times a day—when he first woke up, after he ate lunch, and before he went to bed. He made it a daily routine. The more mindfulness exercises he completed, the more his peace of mind developed. With fewer distractions, he found himself much more productive and confident.

Thank goodness for Mindzone!

With the distractions gone, Austin's happiness bounced back and the drug cravings went away. Mindfulness triggered a positive cycle of change. However, a curious thing happened to Austin towards the end of the week. He noticed the distractions coming back. It happened during a mindfulness exercise one morning. He was trying to focus his awareness when impulsive thoughts entered his mind.

Will I get a job promotion? Will I gain more recognition in the company? Will they give me a pay raise?

These were new distractions disrupting his focus.

Austin exited the freeway, arrived at the arrivals terminal, and scanned the curbside. After a few minutes, he spotted his family waiting for him near the American Airlines Terminal. He got out of his car and hugged his mom.

"We missed you, honey," Claire said.

Austin hugged his father and his sister. He put their luggage in his car and they all hopped in. He asked Isaac to drive them north on the 101 Freeway to San Francisco.

"Son, it's been so long," his father, Dave, said.

Catherine shouted from the back seat. "Where are we going?"

Austin smiled. "It's a surprise."

They drove along the peninsula and looked at the San Francisco Bay. The East Bay was visible in the distance. A few minutes later, they came across a breathtaking view of San Francisco, shimmering under the evening sunset. The Bay Bridge glistened in the distance. Fog was rolling in from the west, and Berkeley was visible to the east. When his family gasped at the magnificent view, he swung his hand across the scene.

"Behold the City by the Bay, the birthplace of the modern information age, where the modern computer and smartphone were first created."

Austin's car drove through San Francisco to the Nob Hill neighborhood and parked near the Fremont Hotel.

Austin pointed. "Mom, we're headed up there."

They looked up to see the Mark Hopkins hotel perched high above Nob Hill. Austin led them into the lobby and up the elevator to the restaurant, "Top of the Mark." Austin and his family sat at a table overlooking the Bay Bridge.

The city view was spectacular. Along its cables, the Bay Bridge gleamed under the evening sky. As the sun set over the horizon, the city lights came on.

Austin pointed through the window. "Let me show you some San Francisco landmarks. That's Coit tower over on that hill. That pyramid shaped building along the downtown skyline is the TransAmerica building."

Dave smiled. "Son, you've brought us to such a beautiful city."

The waiter arrived, and Austin ordered some foie gras and a bottle of an expensive Cabernet Sauvignon from Napa Valley. In a few minutes, the waiter returned and poured their wine.

"Welcome to the Bay," Austin said to his family, picking up his wine glass and toasting them. "I'm sorry I've been so distant recently."

Dave raised his glass. "Thank you, son. Cheers!"

"Wonderful surprise," Claire said.

Austin's parents smiled and they toasted, drinking a sip of the velvety wine. Catherine was too young to drink alcohol. She spent the entire meal looking at her cell phone.

"How are things in school, Catherine?" Austin asked.

Catherine didn't respond, staring at her smartphone.

"Is this normal?" Austin asked his parents.

His mother nodded. "Lately, we've been trying to limit her cell phone use. But for this weekend, we allowed her to use her phone."

Austin waved in front of her sister's face to get her attention. Finally, she looked up. "What?"

"How are things in school?" Austin asked.

Catherine rolled her eyes. "Why do you care?"

Austin ignored his sister. The waiter delivered some appetizers to the table. They tried the foie gras, delicious and smooth, and it went perfectly with the wine.

The waiter came back to take the family's order. "Tonight's specials are duck confit and steak frites, both from Biogastronomy."

Dave looked up. "What's Biogastromony?"

"It's a new company," Austin said. "They make artificial meat in a laboratory, and it's much healthier than real meat."

"Plus it's absolutely delicious," the waiter said.

Dave frowned, making Austin laugh. "Dad, there's a new meat industry in the Bay Area. You don't have to kill animals anymore. Best of all, you spare the animal, but you don't spare the taste."

Dave shrugged. "Well in that case, I guess I'll have to try the duck confit."

"Steak frites for me," Austin said. "Also scallops for my mom and pork sliders for my sister."

Except for his sister's lack of interest, it was a fantastic dinner.

∞ ∞ ∞

The next morning, Austin took his family around the Bay Area. He gave them a tour of Google Headquarters and his department. They visited a futuristic game room with large video screens running the length of the walls. They visited the Google museum and experienced the history of technology. They ate at a spectacular cafeteria with cuisines from all over the world. For Austin's family, Google Headquarters was like a theme park.

After lunch, Austin had an announcement. "This afternoon, I have another surprise. I'm taking you to my sanctuary away from the city."

They drove up the coast and crossed the Golden Gate Bridge, heading north on the 101 freeway. When they left Marin County and entered Sonoma, the fog gave way to sunshine. Soon the first vineyards came into view. They were now in wine country.

"I've always wanted to see Napa Valley," Claire said.

"I know, Mom. That's why I've brought you here."

Austin drove down a side road past several small family wineries. The winding road traversed a river and narrowed into a single lane. Then they came across a black metal gate. "Artesa Winery." The gate opened and they entered.

Artesa was a fortress of wine and modern art built into a Sonoma hillside. From the distance, its main building blended perfectly into its natural surroundings. At the base of the hill was a lake, and sheep grazed all along the hillside. The winery was famous for its modern art and its prized Cabernet Sauvignon, a full-bodied, oaky red wine.

Austin parked his car. "We're almost there. Just have to walk up this hill to the entrance."

Catherine looked up and finally said something. "There's sheep!"

"They're grazing to help the grapes grow."

Austin led them along the path to the winery. Along the way, they stopped and took selfies in front of a fountain. Reaching the top of the hill, they beheld Sonoma County stretching for miles into the horizon.

Austin pointed. "Look, you can see San Francisco in the distance over there."

"Breathtaking," Claire said.

They entered the Artesa winery and a staff member greeted them. "Welcome to Artesa. We are famous for our wine but also for our prized modern art collection. Feel free to walk around while I arrange for your private wine tasting."

Dave looked at the artwork. "This feels like I'm in the New York Museum of Modern Art."

"Except that the art is for sale," Claire replied.

Austin and his family explored the winery and visited its cellar, which smelled like oak barrels. They made their way to an outdoor area, where a private wine tasting awaited them. The sun was shining, and the sky was a deep blue without any clouds in sight. Even the sheep grazing along the hillside were beautiful. Austin was on top of the world.

The family sat at a table in the outdoor patio and waited for their wine tastings, and Austin noticed his sister on her phone. He glanced over and noticed she was using Wired.

"Catherine!" Austin said. "Can you spend just one minute being with us?"

Catherine didn't respond, frustrating her brother. He grabbed the phone away from her and closed her app.

She finally looked at her brother with rage steaming from her eyes. "What's your problem?"

Austin yelled back at her. "You haven't spent a single minute being present with us this entire weekend. You're obsessed with your phone!"

Catherine rolled her eyes.

"How are you doing in school?" Austin asked. "Where are you going to college next year?"

Catherine and her parents were silent.

Austin looked at them.

Something's wrong here.

"Your sister isn't going to college next year," Claire said.

Austin's jaw dropped. "You're not going to college? What are you doing next year?"

"I'm taking a year off and working," Catherine replied. "All my friends are doing the same thing. We're all applying to college next year."

Claire leaned forward. "Your sister was accepted to a private college in Iowa, and we're deciding how we can afford the tuition."

"It's $150,000 per year," Dave said.

Austin shook his head. "But Catherine, you're a straight-A student. They will give you a scholarship."

The family was silent. Austin later learned that in Catherine's junior year of high school, her grades had started to slip. She lost her focus in school, spending most of her time on social media or with her boyfriend.

Austin felt ashamed for not knowing any of this.

I'm so wrapped up in my own life that I don't know my family anymore. What a horrible example I've set for Catherine.

The waiter returned with some wine tastings and appetizers. Upset by his sister, Austin did not think very highly of the wine.

∞ ∞ ∞

After visiting Artesa Winery, Austin drove his family to Napa Valley and toured the area before driving down the 80 Freeway. They stopped at Berkeley and walked along Telegraph Avenue, then visited the University of California at Berkeley. They had dinner at an Indian restaurant and then drove back to San Francisco. By the time the family arrived back home in Sunnyvale, it was almost midnight.

Austin's parents thanked him for the wonderful day trip around the Bay Area. They sat and chatted for a few minutes, and then his parents called it a night and went off to bed.

Austin found himself alone with his sister; he decided to talk to her about her life.

"Catherine, I'm worried about you," Austin said to her.

She seemed confused. "Why do you care about me all of a sudden?"

"Well, I'm worried. You're not going to college?"

"I'll be fine," she said. "A lot of my friends are taking a year off before college. It's the thing to do."

"Why? I don't get it."

"College is really expensive now and not everyone can afford it. Most of my friends went to a university abroad, or they took a year off and worked. It's not just me."

Austin shook his head. "That's a shame. College is expensive now, I know. It's all out of control. Instead of focusing on educating their students, these universities are out to make profits and build research centers. It's so ironic that educating students is such a low priority for them."

"Yeah, it's not like the old days when tuition was cheap. Now college is something for rich people only."

Austin paused and changed the subject. "Catherine, I'm still worried about you. I see you on your phone all the time. I think you're addicted to your phone. Why don't you take a break from it?"

Catherine shook her head. "It's not an addiction, Austin. Don't be stupid."

Austin replied, "Do you know how happy you'll be if you let go of your phone?"

Catherine rolled her eyes.

Austin had an idea. He asked his sister to take a few minutes and join him in a mindfulness exercise. He opened the Mindzone app and the bald man appeared, guided them through a five-minute breathing exercise.

"Today is a new day for peace and happiness," the bald man said with a smile. He instructed them to take a few deep breaths and then focus on their breathing. Catherine closed her eyes and tried to follow the instructions.

Austin closed his eyes and focused on his breaths. However, he could not focus. He wasn't able to clear his

161

mind and focus on the present moment. Thoughts kept racing through his mind. He tried to become aware of the thoughts and realized that all the thoughts were about work.

Why won't they give me a promotion? Why aren't they recognizing my programming? I deserve more than this! This isn't fair!

Austin spent the five-minute exercise trying to maintain focus, but he wasn't able to practice any mindfulness. The thoughts kept coming, interrupting his peace.

The timer went off. Austin and Catherine opened their eyes.

"Well, that was a waste of time," Catherine said, then headed off to bed.

Austin sat alone. He didn't understand what had happened. Just a few days ago, he had felt so much peace and freedom from his daily mindfulness exercises. His distractions had disappeared, and his mind was clear and insightful. Now it seemed his focus was gone.

There were new distractions now. Instead of stocks, drugs, and music, the distractions now related to work, wealth, and promotion.

Austin went to bed feeling upset. He reflected on his life some more, trying to figure what had happened. The answers eluded him.

17.

"**I** MOVE TO HAVE SHIV PATEL removed as Google's CEO."

"We will recess and vote on the motion."

A dreadful tension permeated Google's annual Board of Directors Meeting in New York City. Technology stocks tanked after Congress approved Dabney-Page. Amazon's stock dropped ten percent in one day, bringing Google down for the ride. Investors needed a scapegoat.

Shiv walked towards Ed Koch as the meeting recessed. "Ed, what do you think you're doing? You want to have me removed?"

Ed grinned. "It's all business, Shiv. Nothing personal."

"Personal? How can you say that? I've spent my career growing this company to be the world's largest...."

"Shiv, we've lost $40 billion in market cap since last week. Amazon is gone, and we are next. Our survival is at stake. You just don't get it."

Shiv walked closer. "I made a mistake hiring you, Ed. You are cold-blooded and you've brought no value to this company."

Shiv turned and left the room, heading for a taxi.

This is too much. I need a break.

He entered a Ryde and spoke his destination—The Peninsula Hotel. It was a cold, cloudy day in New York City. With winter a few weeks away, the trees were bare and frigid Arctic air had hit the city.

"Anaya, I'm heading to my hotel for some rest. Notify me ten minutes before the board meeting restarts."

"Okay, Shiv, will you need a taxi back to the event?"

"Yes."

After everything I've done, I can't believe they may force me out.

As the Ryde drove through midtown Manhattan, Shiv spotted protestors and police near the entrance of his hotel. The cab drove down 5th Avenue and turned onto 55th St, where Shiv covered his face and exited the cab, quickly pacing into the Peninsula Hotel.

"Down with Amazon! Down with Google!" the protestors yelled.

A security guard escorted Shiv to his top floor penthouse, where he took off his shoes and crawled into bed, staring at the ceiling.

What have I done to deserve this?

Shiv remembered the words of his father, who told him, "The road less traveled is a lonely one. When you reach Nirvana, there will be no one there to greet you."

Everyone wants to take from me. The ego is everywhere.

A text message arrived.

"Anaya, who texted me?"

"It's from Malia. She says 'Dad, I miss you. Come home.'"

Shiv sobbed. "Anaya, tell Malia I love her."

"Okay, I sent it."

He stared at the ceiling and closed his eyes, practicing a brief mindfulness exercise. A few minutes later, as his core returned to center, an idea came to him.

"Anaya, please open my document about insight."

He looked back at "Awaken the Power of Insight," where he had last written about the ego's grip on the mind. Wherever he looked, he found the ego's footprint.

Ed Koch wants to be CEO. He wants control.

"Anaya, create a new section in this document."

"Okay, what would you like to call this section?"

Shiv sat upright. "Nirvana."

"As you develop awareness through meditation and mindfulness exercises, you will come across the ego, a force that lives within all of us. The ego wants control because it is obsessed about self-survival. Remember, there is no need to have judgments about yourself. Just realize that some of your thoughts come from your ego, a natural part of your development as a human being. When you become aware of the ego, you realize that addictions and selfish desires all come from a central source.

"When you become aware of your ego, ask yourself if it has taken you to a place of happiness. Have the thoughts and emotions from your ego taken you to a state of fulfillment? If your ego's actions give you happiness, how long does the happiness last? Think about these questions during a mindfulness exercise. When you take some time to reflect on your thoughts, you will achieve more insight into your own thought process."

Shiv thought back to the Board of Directors Meeting that morning.

Ed Koch wants to destroy me, but I will not stoop to his level. It's time to discuss the Fourth Noble Truth and the Path to Nirvana.

He continued dictating.

"There is a state of happiness and freedom that is free from the ego's obsessions. Most cultures and religions

165

describe a state of supreme happiness that is separate from superficial self-satisfaction. This happiness does not need constant replenishment because it's permanent. It does not fluctuate with moods or events. Most cultures and religions describe this supreme happiness as coming from love, empathy, and wisdom, all qualities of our inner soul. The development of supreme happiness ultimately arises from the emergence of our soul.

"The soul is in many ways the opposite of the ego. Instead of a worldview driven by self-interest, the soul's worldview accepts the needs of others. The soul places the happiness of others before the happiness of self. The soul does not create divisions or boundaries, but rather understands the unity of the whole. The soul does not make snap judgments based on whether something satisfies the self. Rather, the soul will use wisdom and understanding for decision-making. The soul will place the happiness of others before ourselves, and in so doing give us supreme happiness.

"Reaching Nirvana, the awakened state, means embracing our soul and abandoning the ego. When we finally understand the nature of our world and the common bond among all people, we realize how frivolous and miserable our self-interests truly are. When we replace our selfish worldview with a much larger worldview of humanity, we see the road to Nirvana before us. For people driven by self-interest, the thought of abandoning the ego will seem terribly painful. It takes courage and commitment to become free of the ego's heavy chains. Once there is freedom from the ego, supreme happiness can follow.

"How can someone achieve freedom from the ego and liberate the soul? You may think that the answer lies in suppressing the ego, but that is not the solution. Suppressing our internal compulsions and addictions, or replacing these addictions with new addictions, simply creates conflict. The ego loves to fight and is quick to embrace conflict for its manipulation. Rather than suppressing the ego, the way to achieve supreme happiness is promotion of the soul. By developing awareness of the soul and promoting its presence, we can ensure that its power grows larger than the ego. The soul will naturally replace the ego to become the key driver of thoughts and actions."

Shiv looked from the window. A ray of sunshine broke through the clouds. While a few protestors shouted below, the crowds were now mostly holiday shoppers walking towards a bustling 5th Ave.

"How can we become aware of the soul and increase its presence in our lives? The solution is quite simple. Recall that the subconscious mind is the epicenter of our mental power, and it's also home to the ego and the soul. When we cultivate thoughts in our conscious mind, those thoughts enter the subconscious mind, where they reinforce the ego or the soul. By cultivating thoughts of compassion, we free the soul from the ego's grasp. Our soul will re-enter our lives and guide us."

Shiv thought back to his childhood, remembering a meditation that his father had taught him in high school.

Father's meditation on compassion. I still practice it.

"Anaya, create a new section as follows."

Meditation on Compassion
Step 1 – Set a timer for five minutes and sit on a chair (or on the floor with your back supported).

Step 2 – Begin by taking four slow breaths, and then gently close your eyes.

Step 3 – Become aware of your breath as you inhale and exhale. Notice the moments of silence between the inhale and exhale.

Step 4 – Visualize the word "Compassion" in your mind. Repeat the word to yourself several times.

Step 5 - Think of qualities related to Compassion and meditate on these qualities. These could be kindness, empathy, forgiveness, etc. Whisper each word to yourself and visualize the word. Continue until the timer expires.

"Anaya, continue with dictation."

"Please proceed, Shiv."

"This exercise is a meditation on compassion, an important quality of the inner spiritual self. As you become aware of compassion in your conscious mind, these thoughts of compassion enter your subconscious mind. In the analogy of the conscious mind as a circle, the meditation on compassion is a point within the circle of our conscious awareness. As we meditate on compassion and think of its related qualities, like kindness, empathy, and forgiveness, our subconscious mind reinforces the inner spiritual self, and the soul develops its power in this way."

Shiv drew a circle representing the conscious mind. He then drew two points and connected them with a line. He called his figure "Meditation on Compassion."

Meditation on Compassion

Shiv continued. "Any quality that we send to the subconscious mind will return to us in a moment of need. Let's say an angry classmate or coworker threatens us. Our ego will want to start a conflict, which will only worsen our situation and create additional problems. In general, anger leads to poor decisions and bad outcomes. But when we meditate on compassion, the subconscious mind will remind us to deal with this difficult problem with patience, understanding, and strength. Patience is the best way to deal with anger. In the eyes of the angry foe, your patience and strength will seem like a superpower.

"Compassion is not the only quality that fuels the inner spiritual self. Another quality is devotion, which implies strength, determination, and persistence. Meditating on devotion will also foster the development of the soul. Repeat the five-minute meditation exercise, but instead of meditating on compassion, try meditating on devotion. Think of qualities related to devotion and repeat these qualities to yourself. Later in the day, at a moment of need, the subconscious will remind you to stay strong, patient, and persistent in response to life's challenges.

"You will also benefit from meditating on a third quality. This third quality will also guide your inner spiritual development and empower the soul. Only you know this third quality. It is something you need in your unique life situation. For some people, the third quality may be leadership. For others, it may be patience, communication, or sharing. Choose the quality that is most important for your life, and begin to meditate on it as you have meditated on compassion and devotion. Think of actions related to it. Become aware of this third quality in your conscious mind so that it reinforces your inner spiritual self."

Shiv had an idea. He looked at the previous figure he had made, "Meditation on Compassion." He added several words to the figure – Devotion and Leadership. As with compassion, he drew lines connecting points through the circle. He called this new figure "The Development of the Soul."

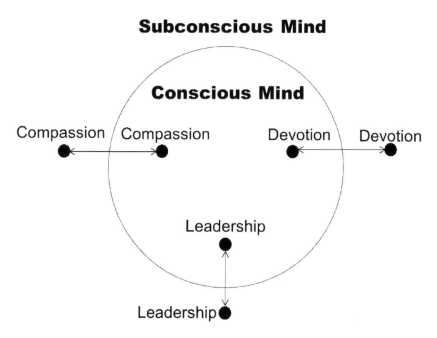

The Development of the Soul

"To develop the soul and transform it into the central driver of your actions and emotions, you can meditate on these three qualities on a daily basis. Let's consider the three traits to be compassion, devotion, and leadership. During a mindfulness exercise, spend a few minutes meditating on each quality, repeating it to yourself and thinking of actions related to it. Then at the end of the exercise, imagine all three traits in your mind. Visualize the three of them in your mind as a triangle."

Shiv drew a triangle connecting the points within the circle. In the middle of the triangle, he drew a large eye, the third eye of awareness. He called his new figure "A Model of Wisdom."

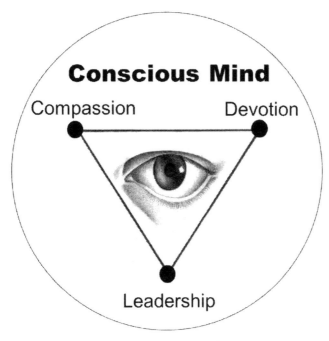

A Model of Wisdom

"Visualize this triangle in your mind, with the words compassion, devotion, and leadership at its points. Imagine yourself maintaining a presence in the triangle. By meditating on these traits, you will communicate to your subconscious mind that they are important for you. As you meditate on these three qualities, you will become aware of the soul. When you face a tough challenge, these three traits will return and guide you through it. Destructive emotions like anger, envy, and greed do not exist in the triangle.

"Your awakened third eye will guide you to a state of wisdom and happiness, where you can realize the highest

171

state of being. Once you rid yourself of the ego's limited vision and poor judgment, you will be free to make decisions that improve not just your own life but also the lives of your friends and family. You will develop wisdom and happiness. What emerges over time is an enlightened mind.

"As your worldview changes from the ego's self-serving view to the soul's worldly view, you will begin to see the divinity within. Feelings of anger, envy, and pride are replaced with compassion, gratitude, and love. We begin to see the love and beauty in people around us, even in people who cannot see it within themselves. The selfless service to others becomes a source of supreme happiness. This is the state of Nirvana, the awakened state, also known as Enlightenment. It is a state of wisdom, compassion, and supreme happiness that arises when you abandon ego, hatred, and greed. Every one of us has the potential to reach the awakened state. Nirvana happens when you become fully aware of the soul within and act for the betterment of the human condition."

"Shiv, your Board of Director's Meeting starts in ten minutes."

"Thanks Anaya."

With a renewed energy, Shiv got up and headed for the lobby, finding no protestors outside his hotel. It was nighttime, the holiday shoppers packing the streets of Manhattan. He stepped into the Ryde that Anaya had ordered and arrived at the St. Regis Hotel in several minutes.

Heads turns to Shiv as he walked in the St. Regis ballroom. He greeted his management and investors with a smile, cutting through the room's cold unease. Ed Koch sat by himself in the corner of the room.

As the meeting reconvened, Shiv grabbed a microphone and walked to the front of the room. "I'd like to say a few words before the committee votes on Ed's motion." The fifty-member audience looked on. "I joined Google in 1999 when it was a fledgling web search company. Back then, Larry and Sergey had no idea their company would one day become the world's largest. We had one goal—to organize the world's information and make it universally accessible and useful. And we had one motto— Don't be evil."

Shiv turned to Ed Koch.

Compassion, devotion, and leadership.

"Google became the world's wealthiest company because we innovated, educated, and accelerated technology. We didn't get here with deceptive business practices, financial engineering, or subversion. We are not Amazon or Microsoft."

A few members of the audience applauded.

"My friends," Shiv said, "we are at a critical crossroads. Other leaders do not see the world as I do. They would rather control and subjugate than advance our common humanity. Let me be perfectly direct with you. The motion to oust me is a motion to change our trajectory. Our principles of compassion and innovation are at stake. If Google abandons its core principles, we face a certain dark ages ahead.

"Dabney-Page is a temporary setback for us. Our stock may face another twenty percent decline, but do not let the jackals take advantage of the situation. Do not be tricked by short-term fear. Look back at our history, and do not abandon Google's core principles. We must continue to innovate, accelerate technology, and bring human beings out of poverty. Our mission is not yet complete."

18.

AUSTIN PLACED THE Bodi smartglasses on his face and opened his Messages App. He was back at work after a weekend with his family. He had dropped his parents and sister off at San Francisco International Airport the evening before.

Through his smartglasses, he scanned his text messages and noticed a new one from Beth. "Looking forward to your next breakthrough."

Austin smiled. He hit reply and dictated a message with his voice. "Working on it."

He took off the smartglasses and thought about his next app.

Why aren't any ideas coming to me?

Austin hit a dead end; the insights were not arriving anymore. Recently, he had lost his focus. Anytime he practiced mindfulness exercises, thoughts raced around his head.

Why can't I innovate? Why do I have so much mental resistance?

Frustrated, he left his cubicle and went for a walk. As he left the building, a cool bay breeze stopped him in his tracks.

This feels so nice.

He went for a morning walk and noticed a large tree. Wanting a few minutes of mindfulness, he sat against the tree trunk in meditative posture. He took out his smartphone and opened the Mindzone App.

The bald man appeared. "Today is another day for peace and success."

Austin glanced at the app's menu and looked through a list of mindfulness exercises. He came across one he had never tried—a meditation on compassion. He clicked on it.

The bald man reappeared. "Let's try a meditation on compassion. Close your eyes and take four slow deep breaths. Then begin by focusing on the sounds around you."

Austin sat cross-legged on the grass and closed his eyes. He took four slow, deep breaths, spending several seconds on each inhale, pausing, and then slowly exhaling the breath. He grew calmer. He focused on the present moment and listened to the sounds around him. He heard a bird crowing in the sky.

After a few seconds of meditation, a slew of thoughts hit Austin. They came in quick succession, one after another. By the time he became aware of one thought, another one interrupted his focus. The thoughts related to work.

Is my Messages App ready for prime time? How can I improve the app? Why did I program face recognition into the app? Is Shiv Patel upset at me?

Austin became aware of the interruptions, labeled the thoughts, and returned to the present moment. He listened to the sounds around him—cars whizzing in the nearby street, birds flying above, an airplane in the distance. Then more thoughts came.

Will I be promoted? What if I can't deliver the next breakthrough? Will I go back to my old ways?

Austin was frustrated. He could not focus on the present moment. He thought about quitting his meditation and going back to the office.

"Let's practice a meditation on compassion," the bald man said. "Imagine the word compassion in your mind. Repeat the word to yourself. Ask yourself what actions constitute compassion. Say these actions out loud to yourself."

Austin paused.

I've never meditated on a word before.

He imagined the word "compassion" in his mind and whispered the word to himself several times. "Compassion." He closed his eyes. "Compassion, compassion, compassion..."

He remembered his visit to Artesa winery with his family. He thought about his sister Catherine. He remembered the love of family, the feeling of togetherness. It was an unconditional love without prerequisites or attachment. As Austin remembered his weekend with his family, a few actions entered his mind.

"Love," Austin whispered to himself. "Empathy, kindness, understanding, tolerance, togetherness..."

"Compassion is the gateway to wisdom and happiness," the bald man said. "It centers the mind and opens the third eye."

Austin's brow relaxed, his tension dissipating.

All I think about is myself – my work, my promotion, my success. I'm so obsessed with myself all the time.

The more he meditated on compassion, the weaker his ego's grip became. He remembered his conversation with Shiv Patel in Beth's office. Shiv had also mentioned compassion as an important attribute.

"Mindfulness by itself won't lead to Nirvana," Shiv had said. "There are other important traits that you need to achieve an enlightened state, such as compassion and devotion."

Sitting there in a grassy field under the large tree, Austin made the connection. Shiv's words came together.

All my desire is creating an immense suffering. Why do I need a promotion? What exactly is a promotion going to give me?

The more he thought about it, the more he realized that the constant desires for promotion and advancement were all unnecessary sources of anxiety.

I'm already working at the best company in the world. My salary is in the top one percent for my age bracket. Millions of people would love to have my job. Why am I so obsessed with getting a promotion?

Austin looked up to the sky and the clouds parted. An insight came to him.

To find a deep happiness, I have to be more appreciative of what I already have.

Relief came over him, a great burden lifting from his shoulders.

I'm happy with my life. I'm proud of who I am now.

The more he meditated on compassion, the more he grew to love himself. The distractions faded, and he found himself back to a state of peace.

Instead of wanting more and complaining about what I don't have, I should start appreciating what I already have.

"Now we will meditate on the important quality of devotion," the bald man said. "Think of devotion. Meditate on this trait. Think of actions that are synonymous with the quality of devotion and say them to yourself."

Austin closed his eyes and tried to mediate on 'devotion.'

Devotion seems religious, and I'm not a religious person. But I suppose devotion applies to me.

"Devotion," Austin whispered to himself. "Devotion means strength, determination, resolve, tenacity, motivation, persistence."

"Devotion is an important quality for anyone," the bald man said, "whether you are a religious scholar, a construction worker, or a rocket engineer. Without devotion, there is no path forward."

Devotion is like an unshakable energy, a deep commitment.

"Lastly," the bald man said, "we will meditate on one final quality. Think of a positive quality you need for your life. Look deep within. Once you have identified the quality, meditate on it and think of actions that equate with this quality."

Austin thought about it for a few seconds.

What quality do I need in my life?

"Innovation," Austin said to himself. He repeated the term several times and contemplated actions equating with it. "New ideas, breakthroughs, insights..."

Austin meditated on 'innovation' for several minutes, looking deep within himself and finding his inner core. He opened his eyes and saw a grassy field and a row of blossoming cherry trees along the walkway. He felt a breeze and listened as it rustled the leaves and branches above. The meditation of compassion worked – his awareness was back.

"Now imagine these three qualities together," the bald man said. "Imagine a triangle with three points— compassion, devotion, and your own quality. Picture yourself within this triangle. Be within this triangle at all times."

Austin closed his eyes and visualized a large white triangle suspended in air. He placed himself inside the triangle. Three words radiated from the triangle's points around him.

"Compassion, devotion, innovation."

Austin imagined himself inside the triangle. He said a prayer to himself, promising to live with these qualities in his heart. Shivers ran down Austin's back as he realized the gravity of the meditation.

I'll open my third eye and use compassion, devotion, or innovation to approach my problems. The triangle will guide me.

He opened his eyes and saw a tree next to him. This was the tree of his rebirth, his own Bodhi tree. A new Austin was born; it was the dawn of a new beginning.

I have to become the leader I'm meant to be.

With the meditation complete, Austin stood and headed back to work. A new wave of energy emboldened him. The insights returned. It was time to take on Project Bodi again.

Austin walked across the grassy field, arrived at his building, and badged in. On his way to his cubicle, he walked past a break room and saw Paul and Jose playing darts. He stopped and greeted them.

Jose gave him a high-five. "How's the *jefe* doing?"

Austin smiled, happy to be among colleagues. "Great, thanks for asking. I'm trying to work on the next app for Bodi."

"What's it going to be?"

"I don't know yet. By the way, I never got a chance to talk to you guys about my app. What do you think of Messages?"

Paul and Jose looked at each other, puzzled.

"Well," Jose said, "do you want my honest opinion?"

Austin laughed. "Yes, of course. I want the app to be the best it can be. Go ahead and tell me your honest opinion."

"I think it needs a lot of improvement," Jose said.

Austin ground his teeth. He felt an instinctive urge to get angry and to defend his territory.

Is that right? Well, let me tell you something...

Austin recognized his ego trying to hijack his thought process. It was a primal anger to defend his turf and control his territory. He remembered Mindzone, and instead of acting on this anger, he became aware of it.

Compassion, devotion, and innovation. I need to release my ego.

He took a few breaths and watched as the anger drifted away.

"Jose, I appreciate your honest opinion," Austin said. "Tell me how to improve the app. I want it to be a winner. After all, we're one company and we should make our products as good as they can be."

Jose seemed surprised. "That's big of you," he said. He paused for a few seconds and then said, "Here's what I think of your Messages app – first of all, the only way people can type in messages is through voice commands. That just isn't practical. What if I'm in a quiet area and I can't speak out loud? Do you really expect people to talk every time they want to send a message to someone?"

Austin nodded. "Yeah sure, I agree. But what's the alternative?"

Paul and Jose looked at each other. Austin sensed their hesitation.

They must be holding something back.

Just then, Austin had an insight – his subconscious mind revealed the way forward.

"Tell you what," Austin said. "If you have an idea to improve the app, I want you to be involved in its development. I will share the credit with you. You can be a co-developer with me."

Jose's eyebrows rose. "What? You want to collaborate? That doesn't sound like the Austin I know."

"Seriously, let's collaborate," Austin told them. "This device might become a breakthrough. For once, let's put our egos aside and work together. If Bodi succeeds, we all succeed, and we might even change the world."

Paul nodded his head. "You're right, Austin. You don't hear that every day around here."

Jose gave a thumbs up. "I'm happy you want to collaborate, Austin. So here's my idea. I've actually been working on it. I think the Messages app needs a keyboard. People should have a way to type their messages and emails."

Austin shook his head. "Keyboard? But why tether a keyboard to the smartglasses? That doesn't sound very practical."

"A virtual keyboard," Jose said. "It's a hologram of a keyboard that projects from a port next to the camera lens. I've worked on holograms for other projects. The keyboard hologram projects onto anything – a desk, a wall, or on the floor. You can even project into empty space right in front of you. With a virtual keyboard, these smartglasses will become a full computer."

Austin's jaw dropped.

This is brilliant. A virtual keyboard will definitely take Bodi to the next level.

Paul spoke up. "A virtual keyboard opens up other possibilities. You can write documents with your smartglasses, something you can't do on a smartphone. We could add Google Docs to Bodi so people can make presentations, spreadsheets..."

"This is a breakthrough," Austin interrupted. "Jose, why don't you integrate your virtual keyboard into my Messages app? I'll add you as a co-developer on the app. We can share the credit."

Jose gave a high-five. "For sure this is a breakthrough! I think we need to collaborate more closely. In fact, maybe we should get the whole team together and brainstorm."

Paul agreed. "That's a great idea. You know I have my own ideas for Bodi."

Austin was in disbelief.

When I put my ego aside and do what's best for Project Bodi, the advancements come on their own.

Austin extended a hand. "Paul, let's hear your idea."

"Well, the other day I was asking myself," Paul said to them. "What feature will differentiate our smartglasses from the smartphone? What would make people throw their smartphones away and wait in line for Bodi?"

Austin and Jose listened intently, waiting for the punchline.

"Google Replay," Paul said.

"What's that?" Austin asked.

Paul continued. "With its camera, the Bodi smartglasses can record everything during the day. We can easily upload two or three days' worth of recorded video into the cloud. With Google Replay, people can go back and watch previously recorded video from earlier in the day."

Austin nodded. "Oh, wow."

"If a student wants to play back a lecture he heard earlier that day, he just opens the Replay App. If someone wants to replay a conversation they had with someone, they just go back and watch it. Now imagine if we apply A.I. and machine learning to all that video in the cloud."

"Brilliant," Austin answered. "You can ask Bodi specific questions about the past."

Paul nodded. "Exactly. You could ask Google Assistant things like, 'Where did I leave my car keys?' or 'What time did my friend ask me to meet him?' If we apply A.I. and machine learning to recorded video, it can quickly analyze the video. The Replay app will get faster over time."

"Wow," Austin remarked, "you will never forget anything ever again. Replay will extend your memory. This app is no doubt a game-changer, and it's only possible with a wearable device."

These people are geniuses. If I put my ego aside and collaborate, the results will be far superior to anything I can accomplish by myself.

"Guys, this is incredible," Austin said. "Why haven't we ever collaborated like this? Let's put our minds together and work as a team. I say we work together in the fourth-floor computer room. I'd like to see this virtual keyboard."

Jose nodded. "Let's do it. I think Kate and Anderson have some good ideas also. I'll ask them to join us."

Paul interjected. "What about Francisco's idea for the Bodi chat app? He's almost finished with his black cube."

Rumors of a mysterious black cube had swirled for months. Supposedly, it could live stream in 360° Virtual Reality, but no one had ever seen the device.

"Ask Francisco to come as well," Austin told them. "In fact, why don't we ask everyone from the team to join us? Let's all work together for once."

They headed up to the fourth floor computer room. They opened the doors and found a dark room with nobody inside. Austin switched on the lights on a massive workspace with over sixty computers and multiple stations carrying tablets and smartphones.

No one's in here. What a waste of an incredible resource.

Austin sat at one of the computer desks.

Let's do something about that.

He turned on the computer and sent an email to the colleagues in his department. "Please come to the computer room upstairs. We are working on some apps for Bodi and would love your input."

Paul and Jose sat at computer stations next to Austin. The three of them coded together, sharing their new ideas. One by one, other colleagues from the department showed up. As new programmers entered the computer room, Austin introduced them to their code of ethics.

"We are all collaborating on Bodi. This is a team effort, and we'll worry about credit later. We need to innovate as one group."

After an hour, there were thirty Google programmers in the computer room, working feverishly on new apps. The enthusiasm was infectious. Soon the room buzzed with conversations, keyboard clicks, and computer sounds.

For the next twelve hours, the team worked feverishly. Hungry and motivated, the programmers unleashed an epic brainstorm with novel concepts. A new set of patents and inventions came to life that afternoon, giving rise to breakthrough apps designed for the world's best Augmented Reality smartglasses.

A synergy of insight arose when Austin and his colleagues put their minds together. History was made in the computer room that day. It was one of the most productive and prolific times in Google's history.

19.

THE ALARM RANG AT 6:00 AM. Beth awoke from a night of sleep next to her husband and child. She turned off the alarm and got out of bed.

She had dreamt that night about Project Bodi. For once, they were pleasant dreams, not the recurring nightmare of standing in front of the EC. Beth got dressed and made a cup of coffee, careful not to awaken Reza and Gabriella. She grabbed her bag and got into her Google SUV.

"Good morning, Beth," Cooper said with a British accent. "It will be cloudy day with a high of sixty degrees."

Beth smiled. "Cheerio, Cooper. Please drive me to work. And play some Thievery Corporation."

Cooper backed out of the garage and headed to Mountain View. It was a fall morning in the Bay Area, with a marine layer drifting from the ocean. The air was cool and crisp. Cooper drove onto the 101 Freeway, which was practically empty at that hour, then headed into Google Headquarters.

"Good morning, Lou," Beth said to the parking attendant.

"Good morning, Dr. Beth."

"It's funny, Lou, the lot seems full today. Usually it's empty at this hour. Is there an event happening on campus today?"

"No, not that I'm aware of, Dr. Beth."

Beth's car drove itself to its reserved parking spot, and she grabbed her bag and walked to her office. Along the way, she practiced a walking meditation, becoming aware of the flowers blossoming along the walkway, the morning dew on the lawn, the smell of freshly cut grass. She badged in to her building.

Inside the building, she found silence and empty cubicles. Puzzled, she entered her office and turned on her computer, finding fifty-seven emails in her inbox. She scanned through them, and one stood out.

"Project Bodi: Quality check pass."

Beth smiled as she read the email. "QC review of Project Bodi – Messages App – No errors discovered. No further revision required. Messages is now approved for company use."

Beth raised her fists.

Bodi's first app is operational! This is terrific news!

Beth checked the rest of her inbox and came across four similar emails. All four had the same subject line but had arrived at different times during the night.

"Project Bodi: Quality check pass."

"Project Bodi: Quality check pass."

"Project Bodi: Quality check pass."

"Project Bodi: Quality check pass."

Beth assumed these were mistakes or duplicate emails. She opened each email and discovered four different submissions to Quality Control—Maps, Chrome, Email, and something called Replay.

Four new apps were designed for Project Bodi? What is going on?

Looking for answers, Beth walked to her employee's cubicles and found them empty. She walked to Sara's cubicle and greeted her assistant as she stretched.

"Good morning, Beth," Sara said to her boss. "Dr. Patel's office called and said they canceled this week's Bodi meeting."

"Oh," Beth replied. "I'll take that as good news."

"I think so. They sense we're making progress."

Beth smiled. "Wonderful. By the way, is there something going on today? The parking lot seems unusually full for some reason."

Sara looked out of the window and shrugged. "Not that I've heard. I think those cars belong to A.I. department employees."

"But no one is at their desks. Where is everyone?"

Sara nodded. "Oh, you haven't heard. Everyone is upstairs in the fourth floor computer room."

"Really? Why haven't they told me?"

Beth left the floor and walked upstairs to the computer room. She opened the door and found the room full of her employees. There were empty pizza boxes and coffee mugs everywhere.

Francisco turned and waved to his boss. "Good morning, Dr. Beth."

"Francisco, what's going on? Are you working on Bodi?"

"You should probably ask Austin."

Beth scanned the room and spotted Austin. She walked over to him and tapped him on his shoulder, startling him. He turned his head and greeted her. "Good morning, Dr. Andrews."

"Hi, Austin," she said with astonishment. "What are you all doing in here?"

"I was planning to tell you but we've been so busy. We're building Bodi's apps. It has been really productive."

"Well that explains the parking lot. Have you spent all night here?"

"Yes, it's our second day here. Some of us are too excited to go home. We're openly collaborating and sharing new ideas."

Beth shook her head. "Austin, how did you do it? I've tried many times to bring people together and collaborate like this, but it has been impossible with everyone's self-serving agendas. I thought most programmers preferred to work alone. What's your secret?"

Austin smiled. "I'll explain, but there's a lot more to tell you. We finished four apps yesterday and you should be getting the quality checks on them. I was going to tell you yesterday. We are all in the zone, and I think we should have an exciting prototype soon."

Beth looked around the room. "This is a pleasant surprise. It's obvious that you're the primary driver of this team, pushing your colleagues to execute their programs. Team building, communication, and coordination—these are all qualities of a leader, Austin. I'm very proud of you."

Jose leaned over, whispering. "The strange part is he's not asking for any credit or recognition. I think something is wrong with Mr. Austin, señora."

Austin laughed. "There's more, Beth. We now have a working keyboard for Bodi. It's a virtual keyboard, and you can direct it onto any surface. It works just like a regular keyboard, except that it's a hologram. It even works in the empty space right in front of you."

Beth shook her head in disbelief.

Is this the same Austin Sanders I placed on probation? How is he leading Bodi's programming efforts? This is impossible.

"Austin, you're doing a fantastic job," Beth said. "I will remove the probation effective immediately. In fact, I think your future here looks very promising."

Austin smiled and stood up to shake his boss's hand. She instead gave him a hug.

"This means so much to me," Austin said. "It's ironic. The less I obsess about my own ego, the more rewards I end up receiving. It reminds me of our conversation with Shiv."

"How do you mean?"

"Well, recently I decided to abandon office politics and do what's best for our team, even if it means less credit for me individually. I checked my ego at the door and decided not to worry about credit or recognition. Ever since that decision, the insights turned on like a firehose."

"Interesting. So letting go of your ego helped you innovate?"

"Definitely. I think the ego is an annoying pest. The best way to innovate is to silence the ego and do what's best for the team."

Beth signaled that she wanted to make an announcement. She walked to the front of the computer room. A silence overtook the room.

"Good morning, everyone," Beth said with a warm smile. "As you know, we have a deadline to complete our final prototype of the Bodi smartglasses. This deadline is seven days away."

Whispers arose.

"I know you've been working hard the last few days. I just want to inform you that Bodi's first app passed its quality control assessments. Messages is officially Bodi's first working app!"

The room erupted in applause.

"I have even better news. Quality Control also approved four new apps for Bodi just this morning. Looks like Bodi has a suite of apps now!"

The applause roared. Jose lifted Austin off the ground and spun him around.

Beth motioned. "Put Austin back down. Let's not injure the star quarterback."

Austin stood on his feet. "This is great news, but I really can't take the credit. We divided and conquered the work, and that's how we implemented so quickly. We have a lot of momentum going into the deadline."

Beth smiled. "This is wonderful. I want to thank Austin for bringing all of you together. I am impressed that all of you are standing up to this challenge as a united team with focus and dedication. And I can't wait to see your final product."

Applause erupted again.

"One thing," Beth said after the applause died down. "One of the apps is called Replay. I'm curious what that's all about."

Austin spoke for the team. "Do you want a demo?"

"In time," Beth said. "For now, I want all of you to maintain your focus and continue developing your apps. In seven days, we have an Executive Committee meeting where we will unveil our final device. What we present will depend on what you can deliver in the next seven days. Let's stay in the zone. We can make history right here in this room."

With those words, Beth walked off and headed back to her office, kicking her heels on the way.

This is all Austin's doing. He definitely deserves a promotion and greater visibility in the company.

In the ensuing few days, the A.I. department worked feverishly to complete Bodi's Tensorflow code and its apps. Not a single person in the department complained of working late hours. They were a motivated, united team with a common purpose.

In only a matter of days, the A.I. department managed to program an entire library of apps. There were apps for emails, web browsing, online shopping, and movie streaming. There were new games and social media apps designed specifically for smartglasses. A new app, Chat, allowed you to video chat in a far more interactive way than video chatting on a smartphone or computer.

On November 4, 2029, Beth emailed a message to the Executive Committee. "On Tuesday, come see what we have in store – A.I. Dept."

20.

"**W**ELCOME EVERYONE TO the Executive Committee meeting."

It was the first Tuesday in November, 2029, the official deadline for Project Bodi. As the senior management filed in, Shiv Patel sneered when Ed Koch walked into the room. A palpable tension presaged the event.

Shiv opened the meeting and introduced the day's guests – Dr. Bethany Andrews and her programmer, Austin Sanders. "It was exactly nine weeks ago that I announced our challenge to develop the Bodi smartglasses. While it was a difficult undertaking, Beth's team managed to submit their final prototype just two days ago."

Shiv made eye contact with Ed.

I'm ready for you this time.

Beth and Austin sat in front of the Executive Committee. On the table in front of them were twelve unlabeled cardboard boxes.

Beth began her presentation. Slide one appeared on a blank screen in front of the committee. "Project Bodi: The First AR + VR Smartglasses."

"Before we begin," Shiv said to the committee, "I just want to thank Beth and her department for their hard work and dedication. I will admit that this was a difficult challenge. The timelines were strict and deliverables were of high expectation. There were many hurdles the team had to navigate."

Beth responded. "Thank you, Shiv. I also have to thank my staff for their dedication. In particular, I have to thank Austin Sanders for a number of insights that were critical for Bodi's development. Austin was also instrumental in bringing the team together to meet today's deadline."

Austin blushed. He made a nervous gesture and bowed his head in front of the committee.

Beth continued. "Today we will introduce the prototype of the Bodi smartglasses. We are confident of a 2030 product launch. The final product will be called Google Vision."

Beth paused. "Bodi is the first pair of smartglasses with integrated AR and VR capabilities. It's a first in many other ways – the first pair of smartglasses with a visual command platform and the first with eye tracking technology. It also has ground-breaking Augmented Reality apps specifically designed for the platform."

Eyebrows rose. Roger put down his smartphone.

Beth moved to slide two. "We are confident that adoption of AR will cause a major paradigm shift. We estimate that 30-40% of smartphone users will immediately adopt smartglasses as their primary mobile device. There is the potential for a massive disruption in the tech space."

Ed Koch interrupted. "How did you arrive at 30-40%? It seems rather high."

"That's based on feedback from marketing," Beth said. "The only way to truly gauge that is to see the final product. And that's why we are here."

Beth and Austin stood and distributed the cardboard boxes to the Executive Committee members, then returned to their table. Austin sat back down and Beth remained standing.

"I have only three slides in my presentation," Beth said. "Here is slide three."

Beth advanced to slide three, an acknowledgement slide listing everyone who had participated in the Bodi effort. It was a long list of Googlers from multiple departments. Austin's name was at the top of the list.

"And with that, I'm finished with my presentation. Please go ahead and open your boxes."

Shiv smiled. He looked down and picked up the cardboard box. "It's very light." He opened the box and found a smaller white box inside. The front of the white box was transparent, and he could see a pair of smartglasses.

Shiv opened the white box and picked up the Bodi smartglasses, rotating them and inspecting them in the air. "Spectacular!" he said, turning to Ed.

It looked like a pair of black Ray-Ban sunglasses, sleek and modern with "Google" written on a side frame. There was a small camera hole on the front bridge of the glasses. Next to the camera hole was a second smaller hole. There was an on/off button on the right rear earpiece of the smartglasses. The lenses were slightly tinted. Shiv placed the glasses on his face.

Roger palmed the glasses. "So light! No outward sign of the massive computing power in the frames."

Beth smiled. "Exactly right. The first thing you'll notice is how sleek and modern they feel. We wanted a cool device, something people would love to show off. Style was very important in our design."

"I'm already impressed," Roger interrupted, "and I haven't even seen the functionality!"

Beth took her time and allowed the committee to explore. "There is an on/off button here on the back of the glasses," she said, pointing to a small black button on the right rear earpiece. "Go ahead and turn on the device."

Shiv turned on his smartglasses and placed them back on his face. A "Google" icon appeared in front of him in 8K video resolution. The "Google" icon then disappeared, and a new window popped up. At the top was a sign: "Welcome to Google Vision." Below it, the following appeared: "As you look around, Google Vision will track your eye movements."

As Shiv read the welcome screen, a female voice introduced the smartglasses through two small speakers on the earpieces. "Welcome to Google Vision. This device tracks your eye movements, and there are two ways to click on icons or objects in your view. You may now customize your device."

Two images appeared on the screen—a bullseye and a closed eye.

"Please choose how you would like to select objects," the female voice said. "You can select objects by staring at them for one second or by blinking at the object. Please choose one option now. If you need to change your option at a later time, please go to your 'Settings' tab."

Beth spoke up. "After you turn on your device, you'll come to a welcome screen that prompts you to customize your device. Follow the instructions and then you'll get to your home screen."

Shiv chose the first option – clicking on objects by staring at them for one second. He stared at the bullseye for one second, and then a green checkmark appeared. The welcome sign disappeared, replaced by the device's home window—a blank screen with the date and time in the upper right corner. He noticed a row of small icons at the top left corner of the screen. Everywhere his eyes looked, a small white cursor followed.

It feels like I'm using a mouse but with my own eyes. This is a new and exciting feeling!

Beth continued. "Once you get to the home screen, you will notice some icons on the top left corner of your view. If you're looking straight ahead, you probably will not see the icons, so you may have to look up and to the left. These are your apps and settings icons. If you'd like to further personalize your settings, you can do so in the settings tab."

Shiv wasted no time and explored the apps. He stared at the Email app icon, and an email inbox appeared on the left side of his view. It appeared to be a generic inbox for a fictitious person. He clicked on an email from someone named "Rod" and the full email having something to do with delivering appliances appeared on the right side of his screen.

Shiv noted "reply," "reply all," and "forward" tabs at the bottom of the email. "Beth," he said aloud, "how do we compose text in this device?"

Beth smiled. "I see you've moved on to the next step. Austin, please show our committee how to compose text in Bodi."

Austin grew pale. He took a deep breath and gathered himself, then stood in front of the committee. "Yes...composing text. Well, when you select a text field, you will notice that a keyboard pops up in your view. You can stare at the keyboard and select one letter at a time, which is obviously a slow process. We've designed other ways to type text more quickly. First, you can dictate your message with your own voice. Or even better, you can use a virtual keyboard."

Amy Fishman looked up. "What's a virtual keyboard?"

Austin nodded. "The best way is to see it for yourself. Please go to the settings tab and select the 'virtual keyboard' option."

Wasting no time, Shiv navigated to his icons on the top left corner of the screen and opened the settings tab.

Under "Keyboard," he selected the "Virtual Keyboard" option. Then he navigated back to the Email app and opened the email from Rod. After hitting "Reply," he went to type in text when a hologram of a keyboard appeared in front of his face.

What the heck is this?

It was a white keyboard made of light. Wherever he moved his head, the keyboard followed. Shiv placed it on the desk in front of him and typed an email to Rod, then clicked "Send."

Impressive device. Very intuitive. The apps feel organic, like an extension of the human mind.

Shiv opened Messages and played around with it, sending text messages to fictitious people. He checked to make sure there was no face recognition technology embedded in the app.

This is a much faster way of sending text messages than the smartphone.

"Beth," Shiv said. "Do I have to be in the Messages app to receive messages? It's a bit of a hassle to toggle back and forth to Messages."

Beth turned. "Good question. A red Messages icon notifies you of a new text message, and you can further customize your notifications in Settings."

Shiv nodded. He continued to explore the device. He opened Chrome, the web browser, and surfed several websites. He loaded the CNN website and saw the headline: "Hurricane Eileen nearing New York City." The pictures and video streamed rapidly in 8K resolution.

Beth continued. "Maps is a great app. When you open Maps, a prompt will ask you to enter a destination. When your destination is set, the navigation cues appear in your field of view and update as you travel. Navigating in Bodi is far more convenient compared to a smartphone. Just follow the arrows and cues that show up on your screen."

Beth paused for a moment. "Also, in Maps there's an AR search and review feature. Let's say you are looking for a coffee shop. Enter 'coffee shop' in the search field and instantly all of the nearby coffee shops will pop up in your field of view. You can look around and see the coffee shops in your immediate vicinity. You can check their reviews and ratings and even pre-order a coffee through the smartglasses. If you're old-fashioned and want to search on a 2D map, you can configure that in the settings tab."

Shiv opened the Maps app and typed in his home address, and a white icon appeared in the corner of his eye. It pointed in the direction of his home. After clicking on the icon, navigation instructions to his home appeared in his view.

This is a completely new way of interacting with the environment. It really feels like Augmented Reality.

"There's more," Beth said. "There's a feature in Maps that lets you explore your environment. Say you're walking down the street and see a new restaurant. In the Maps app, you can select that restaurant to learn more about it. Check reviews, make a reservation, see the menu – all in a few seconds through the smartglasses. It's a more natural way of exploring your environment compared to the old smartphone."

Shiv stood up and walked towards a window. While in Maps, he looked out and saw a Starbucks in the distance. He looked at the store for one second and an icon popped up. When he stared at the icon, a small box appeared: "Starbucks, 1380 Pear Ave., Mountain View, CA." The coffee shop had a four-star rating, and all of its contact information and reviews were shown.

It feels like I have some new kind of X-ray vision. I can get more information about anything I look at!

He spotted a building across campus and stared at it for one second and an icon appeared: "Google

Headquarters." He turned and stared at an outdoor concert hall: "Shoreline Amphitheatre."

Beth commented. "The search and review feature is only possible when you've opened the Maps app. This way you can enter this 'discovery' mode by your own choice."

Beth waited for Shiv to sit back down, and then she continued. "Another app I love is Shopping," she said. "That's the app with a shopping cart on its logo. In this app, you can shop for anything in your field of view."

Shiv opened the Shopping app. A search field appeared at the top of the screen. Whenever Shiv looked at an object in his view, he received a prompt to order it online. He looked at his watch for one second, and an icon appeared with the name of the watch, its designer, reviews, price, and option to purchase.

I can order anything I look at!

"In the Shopping App," Beth said, "you can also choose to shop the old-fashioned way, like you would on a smartphone. You can search for items by their names, scan any bar code, run price matching, and access your previous orders."

I need to order an electric car charger. Let's test this out.

Shiv clicked on the search field and used the virtual keyboard to type "car charger." Within a second, there were listings for chargers of all shapes and sizes. He clicked on "Rapid car port charger" and then selected "checkout." The process took a matter of seconds.

This is incredible!

"I'm impressed," Shiv said to the team. "I think these smartglasses are a breakthrough. This exceeds my own expectations. You guys have done a fantastic job."

Beth smiled. "Thank you, Shiv, but we're not even half way done with the features! There are all sorts of apps and games. One app I'm really fond of is Google Replay."

Shiv went back to the home screen and spotted the Replay app. He opened the app and several items appeared in his field of view: "Play" and "rewind" buttons, a search field, and a clock.

"Please open the Replay app," Beth said. She waited for everyone to catch up. "This app allows you to replay events from the last 72 hours. We have uploaded all the video recorded by the device's camera into the cloud. So now you've got your own personal video recorder you can access anytime."

Shiv chuckled. He clicked the rewind button and it took him back in time to the beginning of the meeting. He watched as Beth introduced Austin and advanced to slide two. He moved the clock and fast-forwarded the video.

These innovations are extraordinary.

Beth continued. "When you first open Replay, you will notice a clock, a search field, and play and rewind buttons. You can move the clock back to any time in the past 72 hours and replay video from your past. A student can go back and watch a college lecture. You can 'rewind the time' to make sure that you locked the doors to your home this morning."

Roger and several other Executive Committee members cheered. "This is something else," Roger said. "I can't remember the last time this committee got excited over something. We're a bunch of type A executives who rarely ever smile at these meetings."

"Speak for yourself," Amy Fishman replied.

Beth moved on. "About the search feature in Replay," she said. "We are integrating machine learning into the app. With that functionality, you will be able to ask specific questions about the past. You can ask Replay anything: Did I lock the house? Where did I park my car? Google Assistant will search the videos in the cloud and answer your questions. It can even take you to those moments so you can review the video yourself."

Ed Koch removed his smartglasses. "Shiv, this feature is concerning. There will be immediate public backlash against Google Replay. I can already see the lawsuits. I motion that we stop Project Bodi's development and assess the impact."

Shiv's brows furrowed. "Here we go again, Ed. If we had listened to you nine weeks ago, we wouldn't be standing here with this revolutionary device. You are an obstacle to innovation."

Ed stood his ground. "Look at the polls. People are worried about A.I. taking over."

"No," Shiv said flatly. "I'm not concerned about any public backlash. For twenty years, I've been hearing that A.I. will 'take over' society. Even smart people like Elon Musk were afraid of A.I. All that fear-mongering was complete bullshit."

"Bullshit? I read an article that A.I. robots are five years away..."

"You don't get it, Ed. With these A.I. advancements, man is still in control. The technology will improve our lives, not control it."

Ed gave a stone-cold stare. "I propose we hold a vote to stop development of Project Bodi."

Shiv laughed. "Last week you tried to oust me at the Board of Director's Meeting. Your vote fell short then and it will fall short again today. Who votes to stop Project Bodi? Please raise your hand."

Ed's hand rose. He looked around and found no one else raising their hands. A few seconds later, he grabbed his belongings and left the room.

Shiv faced the remaining committee. "Google is great because we innovate. We motivate our employees to be the best they can be, and we reward them for their risk-taking. I stand by Beth and Austin. They are my heroes, and I will do everything I can to empower them."

Roger nodded. "Our greatest assets are our employees."

"That's right," Shiv said. "We must engage our employees. Group insight is a powerful force capable of extraordinary achievements. Look at the Manhattan Project, man's first flight to the moon, and the Genome Project, all breakthroughs where people united and collaborated with a common purpose."

"And soon we will add Project Bodi to that list," Roger said.

The room quieted. Beth gave the committee some time to explore their smartglasses. She spoke up a few minutes later. "Don't forget one other important feature – Virtual Reality. Bodi is a powerful VR device. You can enter VR mode by clicking on its icon in the apps menu."

Shiv looked up at his menu list and opened the "VR" app. His view darkened and a search field appeared. He paused, then typed in "rollercoaster" and selected the top search result.

Suddenly Shiv was in a rollercoaster, slowly climbing up a ramp, and he saw a steep drop-off in the near distance. He looked around to see a theme park below. Screams and laughter came from the people around. As the rollercoaster completed its climb, it slowly began to descend.

Then the drop came.

Shiv's heart sank as he flew towards the earth, hurtling forward at high speed. He shut his eyelids and grimaced, then took off the smartglasses after only a few seconds.

"What happened?" Roger Niles asked him.

"Rollercoaster," Shiv replied frantically.

They laughed together like children.

Beth interrupted the group. "I forgot to mention one important app. Google Chat is an incredible experience on the Bodi smartglasses. It is the most immersive video chat ever created."

She reached into a box and pulled out a small black cube, placing it on the desk in front of her.

"Please open the Chat app," Beth said.

Through the smartglasses, Shiv spotted the Chat app and opened it. A contact list and a prompt appeared.

It's asking me who to chat with.

"Once you've opened the Chat app," Beth said, "please select my name from the contact list."

Shiv looked through the contact list and selected "Bethany Andrews." Beth appeared a few feet away from him. He looked around and waved at her.

That black cube is a camera.

Beth explained. "This black cube allows recording in 360 degrees, or Virtual Reality. You are looking at me through the camera in this black cube. If I move this black cube around, you will see that your video feed also moves along with it. Just keep watching as I place the black cube up on this window sill."

Shiv moved through space as Beth moved the black cube and placed it on the window. He could now see the view from the window, spotting the Starbucks from before.

Shiv interrupted. "Beth, this is incredible. But what are you seeing from your view?"

"Good question," she said. "Right now I see twelve requests to chat. Let me go ahead and accept your request, Shiv." She paused briefly. "Well, now I see the view of the room from your smartglasses. You see, since you don't have a black camera cube connected to your device, it defaults to your camera. Austin, can you connect a camera to Shiv's smartglasses?"

Austin placed a black camera cube in front of Shiv and connected the device wirelessly.

"Thanks Austin," Shiv said. "Beth, are we connected?"

Beth moved her black cube to her desk in front of her. "Yes, Shiv, I can see you through your black cube."

Shiv laughed. "What an incredible video chat. I can see everything around you. And if I turn my head around, I can see the back of my own head!"

"Yes, Google Chat is a groundbreaking app," Beth said. "It not only runs VR video chatting in real time, but it also live streams in 360° Virtual Reality. Imagine live streaming your wedding or the birth of your child for your family to see."

Shiv nodded. "Yes, this is next-generation VR. People can now live stream in 8K resolution. The possibilities for this technology are infinite. I can hardly grasp where this technology will lead us. It's the birth of a new era."

"We think so," Beth said. She went on to describe other features of the Bodi smartglasses, including customization—how you could personalize apps and tailor the home page layout for your needs. She explained how to add weather, news, and other information to the home screen, how to drag and drop items around the screen, and how to apply updates and load new apps onto the device. Her presentation lasted another hour.

As Beth wrapped up her presentation, she remembered one final agenda item before opening the floor to questions.

"One more thing," Beth said, a reference to Steve Jobs, the pioneer of the smartphone. "Austin Sanders has designed one final app that he would like to introduce."

Austin closed his eyes and took a deep breath. He stood up in front of the committee. "Thank you, Beth. Yes, there is one additional app that I've designed, and I'm proud to introduce it. It was actually inspired by Beth."

Austin paused for a moment. "The app is called Google Zen. It's an app for guided meditation and mindfulness. Please go to the app list on your home screen and open the Zen app."

Shiv went back to his home screen and looked at his app list, searching for Zen. He found it. The logo on the Zen app looked like this:

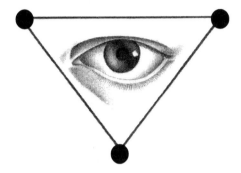

Shiv opened the Zen app and a menu opened. It was a list of mindfulness exercises. There was a listening meditation, a breathing meditation, a noting meditation, a compassion meditation, and several others. Shiv clicked on the breathing meditation and a ten-minute mindfulness exercise began.

"Interesting," Shiv said to Austin. "What was your inspiration to create this app?"

Austin smiled. "Beth introduced me to meditation a couple of months ago. She recommended the Mindzone app. I started to practice the daily meditations, and after a few weeks, I noticed a big difference. It really changed my life. My mind became free of distractions. And I became smarter and more confident. The more I quieted my mind, the more insight I developed."

Beth smiled in pride.

"So to answer your question," Austin said, "I developed the Zen app to give people the chance to discover the power of meditation and mindfulness. As you yourself said, these techniques are thousands of years old, but they work even today. I want people to know that there is a deep power in their mind. It's the subconscious mind. If people can access their subconscious mind through meditation and mindfulness, they can unlock their mind's true potential."

Shiv nodded his head. "You are absolutely correct, Austin. This device is a real breakthrough. Congratulations to the A.I. department and to us as one company. Google Vision will change people's lives forever. However, as the guardians of the biggest company on earth, we have an obligation to make sure this technology does not create problems, distractions, and addictions for people. Austin, I see your app as part of that obligation to our society."

The committee agreed.

"Addiction to information is a serious addiction," Shiv said. "We have to ensure that people become aware of their addictions and get help if they need it. Technology used for good purposes can take human beings beyond their potential and into the next realm. However, technology used for bad purposes can cripple our brothers and sisters. We must have compassion and love for all human beings and for our society. We must ensure that our products are used for the betterment of all people."

The Committee grew quiet, absorbing their CEO's words. Shiv Patel's ideas reverberated across the group, and they would soon reverberate across the world. Compassion, devotion, and innovation where the attributes that he lived by. They were the traits of a Bodhisattva, a person who lives with great compassion for the advancement of all human beings, one who is on the way to becoming a Buddha.

"Thank you for your kind words," Austin said.

Beth stood up next to Austin. "With that," she said, "our presentation is complete. We can open up the floor to any questions."

The Executive Committee members stood up and applauded. It lasted for several minutes.

Beth turned around and hugged Austin.

It was the happiest moment of his life.

EPILOGUE

O N JUNE 1, 2030, at a highly publicized debut at Google Headquarters in Mountain View, the public finally got a chance to see the Google Vision smartglasses. Rumors of its release had been swirling for months. There were images and proposed sketches of the device circulating around the Internet. It would be the biggest unveiling of a tech device since Steve Jobs introduced the iPhone in 2007.

The product unveiling was broadcast around the world. Hundreds of media organizations, news outlets, and tech blogs covered the event, which occurred in a large attendance hall on Google's main campus. However, most news outlets found themselves in a large grassy field behind the attendance hall. Only a few hundred lucky guests were allowed inside the venue.

It was one of the most significant events in American History. Google Vision ushered in a new era of wearable technology, and it transformed how people interacted with the world and with each other. Not only that, it also transformed the human mind itself. With smartglasses, people became smarter, faster, more innovative, and more capable than ever before. It was the next paradigm shift in the information technology age.

Google sold 100 million Google Vision smartglasses in the first year of its release. Approximately ten percent of all smartphone users adopted the smartglasses in 2030. That number grew to fifteen percent in 2031, twenty percent in 2032, and thirty percent in 2033. Unable to compete with Google's breakthrough device, Apple filed for bankruptcy in 2033, another testament to what happens to companies that no longer innovate. Apple's last product was the iPhone 18, just another smartphone with the same old features.

In 2033, Google was worth more than the next 499 richest companies combined. With this rise in Google's power came an important social obligation to maintain free information and continue to improve society's wellbeing. As long as Google's CEO led with compassion, devotion, and wisdom, the future of the world looked bright.

Austin Sanders was promoted to manager just a few months before Google Vision's release. He hired two programmers and continued to work on apps for the smartglasses. He redesigned the Zen app several times, adding new features and designs. He designed groundbreaking mindfulness exercises that could not have been imagined by the Buddhists of long ago.

A few weeks after Google Vision launched, Austin asked his girlfriend Olivia to marry him. They tied the knot at a ceremony at the Artesa Winery in Napa, California. Austin also asked his sister Catherine to live with them for a few months, and he even convinced her to apply to college. The following fall, Catherine enrolled at the San Francisco State University as a college freshman.

In 2030, Austin was promoted to senior manager. He discovered a peculiar thing. Anytime he cultivated his inner eye of awareness and wisdom, he received the insights for the next big breakthrough. However, every time the insights came and he designed the next breakthrough, his ego would surface, tempting him with emotion, money, and desire. As soon as he gave in to his ego, the insights vanished and he went back to a state of ignorance. Then he would have to start the process over and develop his soul all over again.

It was a cyclical process. Austin went back and forth between his ego and his soul. He realized that he could never get rid of his ego; it was a natural part of his being. However, by understanding the dynamics between the ego and soul, Austin understood the essence of his mind. He learned that the ego and soul were intimately involved in the human character. They were the yin and yang of the human experience.

By understanding how the ego and soul worked, Austin unleashed a creative wave of energy that lasted for decades. He continued to innovate even into old age, far longer than any of his colleagues. He was rewarded at every step with awards and promotions. He was quickly promoted from Senior Manager to Vice President and then to Senior Vice President.

Shiv Patel's book, "Awaken the Power of Insight," was published in 2030 and immediately rose to number one on the New York Times Bestseller list. However, there was backlash against the book by many in society who argued that Google's power was too great. Shiv donated all proceeds of the book to helping young people with addiction. He started a scholarship for students with disadvantaged backgrounds, helping thousands of young people attend college.

In 2033, Bethany Andrews received the National Medal of Science for her work related to Google Health. At her ceremony, the President of the United States called Dr. Andrews "the most brilliant mind of the century." She was humbled by the President's words and asked that he call her "Beth."

Beth continued to work tirelessly to develop the next breakthrough that would move society forward to its highest potential. In 2055, Google's Board of Directors unanimously selected Beth to be Google's CEO. She chose Austin Sanders to be her Senior Vice President and head of the A.I. Department. In 2056, in response to a new global climate threat, they initiated a new project that would one day take humanity deep into the frontiers of space.

THANK YOU

for reading Project Bodi. Please submit a review of the book on its Amazon, Goodreads, and Facebook pages.

http://viewbook.at/bodi

https://www.facebook.com/projectbodi

https://www.goodreads.com/book/show/37859985-project-bodi

EXERCISES

Breathing Exercise

Step 1 – Set a timer for five minutes, sit on a chair, and close your eyes.

Step 2 – Begin by taking a slow inhale and count for four seconds. Hold the breath for four seconds, and then exhale your breath for four seconds. This is one complete breath.

Step 3 – Count each breath at the end of each exhalation. Count these breaths from one to ten.

Step 4 – Once you've finished counting ten breaths, start over from the first breath. Continue counting breaths until the timer expires.

Noting Exercise

Step 1 – Set a timer for five minutes and sit on a chair (or on the floor with your back supported).

Step 2 – Begin by taking four slow breaths, and then gently close your eyes.

Step 3 – Mentally scan your body starting from your head and slowly moving down to your toes. Notice any sensations or discomforts in each part of your body.

Step 4 – Anytime you are interrupted by a thought or emotion, become aware of it. Analyze the thought or emotion without any judgment. Label it as a "thought" or an "emotion" and give it a quality ("positive" or "negative"). Watch the thought or emotion until it disappears.

Step 5 – Continue to mentally scan your body until the timer expires.

Mindfulness Exercise

Step 1 – Set a timer for five minutes and sit on a chair (or on the floor with your back supported).

Step 2 – Begin by taking four slow breaths, and then gently close your eyes.

Step 3 – When something in your environment gets your attention, such as sound or a physical sensation, focus your attention on it. Maintain your presence in the now.

Step 4 – Anytime you are interrupted by a thought or emotion, become aware of it with wakeful attention. Identify the thought or emotion and give it a quality ("positive" or "negative"). Do not have any judgments of yourself. Simply watch the thought or emotion until it disappears.

Step 5 – Return to step 3 and continue until the timer expires.

Focused Meditation

Step 1 – Set a timer for five minutes and sit on a chair (or on the floor with your back supported).

Step 2 – Begin by taking four slow breaths, and then gently close your eyes.

Step 3 – Clear your mind and meditate on the first thing that enters your mind. It could be a person, an emotion, or a thought. Focus your mind on this object for a few minutes.

Step 4 – Allow your focus to naturally move to your breathing or hearing when appropriate.

Meditation on Compassion

Step 1 – Set a timer for five minutes and sit on a chair (or on the floor with your back supported).

Step 2 – Begin by taking four slow breaths, and then gently close your eyes.

Step 3 – Become aware of your breath as you inhale and exhale. Notice the moments of silence between the inhale and exhale.

Step 4 – Visualize the word "Compassion" in your mind. Repeat the word to yourself several times.

Step 5 - Think of qualities related to Compassion and meditate on these qualities. These could be kindness, empathy, forgiveness, etc. Whisper each word to yourself and visualize the word. Continue until the timer expires.

Third Eye Meditation

Step 1 – Set a timer for five minutes and sit on a chair (or on the floor with your back supported).

Step 2 – Begin by taking four slow breaths, and then gently close your eyes.

Step 3 – Meditate on "Compassion." Repeat the word, visualize it, and think of its related qualities.

Step 4 – Meditate on "Devotion." Repeat the word, visualize it, and think of its related qualities.

Step 5 – Meditate on a third quality that's important for your life. Repeat the word, visualize it, and think of its related qualities.

Step 6 – Repeat all three qualities to yourself. Imagine a triangle where each point represents a quality. Picture yourself within the triangle. Open your third eye.

Made in the USA
San Bernardino, CA
27 May 2018